To Kelly,
Thanks for the
support!
Crystal V. Rhodes

SWEET SACRIFICE

Other Books by Crystal Rhodes

Sin

A woman minister, renown in her community for her anti-drug activism, falls in love with a man who unknown to her is involved in the drug trade.

Sin can be ordered online at
http://www.genesis-press.com,
or at Amazon.com.
(Genesis Press, ISBN #1-58571-017-2)

SWEET SACRIFICE

a novel by

Crystal Rhodes

CRYSTAL INK Publishing
Indianapolis, Indiana

SWEET SACRIFICE

Published by CRYSTAL INK Publishing
P.O. Box 53511
Indianapolis, Indiana 46253

This is a work of fiction. All events, characters, places and incidents are strictly products of the author's imagination. Any similarities to persons living or dead are completely coincidental.

Printed in the United States

ISBN: 0-9719586-1-0

Library of Congress Catalog Card Number:

2002092273

DEDICATION

This book is dedicated to the four women who have influenced my life the most: my mother, Betty Ann Rhodes, my grandmother, Hattie Williams and my aunts, Virginia Clarke and Florabelle Wilson, and to my daughter, Nailah, who continues the legacy of strength and endurance. I'm glad that she is a part of my life.

ACKNOWLEDGEMENTS

I would like to extend a warm thank you to Joni Clarke, whose editing, suggestions and support has been invaluable, as I've traveled through this writing journey.

A big thank you to Eunice Revis-Butler and Lillie Barnett Evans who extended their editing expertise over the years.

Also, a big kiss and hug for my cousin, Peter Clarke. I love you cuz. Thanks for always being there.

A thank you goes out to author, Delores Thornton, who has selflessly offered me guidance and the benefit of her experience.

Finally, a warm thank you and love forever to my Aunt Florabelle for your love, support, encouragement, assistance... I could go on and on.

PROLOGUE

Sash Adams closed the small notebook and tucked it back inside her leather boot when she heard the key click in the lock. With her heart pounding and her palms sweating, she sprang from the bed and positioned herself behind the door of the tiny room. Gripping her gold-plated pen tightly in her right hand, she used her left hand to support her balled right fist. Poised like a grotesque statue frozen in granite, she stood waiting, ready to attack.

The door opened and her captor appeared in the doorway. The split second it took him to turn and face her was all that she needed to strike. The look of surprise on his face made her next move easy. He was short, about five feet five. They stood almost eye to eye as she sprang forward, propelled by the adrenaline pumping through her system. Instinctively, he jerked backward raising his hands to protect his face. The movement deflected the pen from his face, but the sharp point sliced through the fleshy underside of his arm. Yelping in pain the man staggered backward as blood oozed from the wound in his arm. Sash wasted no time as she struck again.

Mustering all of the leverage that she could, Sash retained

her deathlike grip on the pen and in one single movement plunged it deeply in the man's slightly protruding stomach. He screamed and staggered backward, struggling to stay on his feet and propelling Sash forward with him. Tottering, she managed to stay on her feet, but was determined to see him fall.

Drawing her foot back, she aimed for his groin and with as much force as she could manage landed a direct hit. Doubling over he fell to his knees. A second kick beneath his chin forced his head backward, a third kick sent his body crumbling to the floor. Mission accomplished. He lay on the floor bloody and moaning.

Leaping over the man who lay between her and freedom, Sash raced out of the room that had become her dreaded prison into a second room where another closed door, only a few yards, away stood as a barrier. With a tug of confidence, she pulled on the doorknob. It was locked.

Swiftly, Sash's eyes examined the door. It was old, fragile; the wood was aged and cracked. Unlike the former door that contained a deadbolt, the lock on this door was an older, single cylinder lock that required a key. She was sure that her moaning captor had it in his pocket; but there was no time to search—no time to waste. The door had to be opened *now*.

Bracing herself, Sash kicked the door with one booted foot, using every ounce of her 125 pounds for momentum. The force of her efforts sent her staggering backward, but she remained standing as the sound of splintering wood was followed by a blast of cool air on her sweat drenched body. The wooden door now stood open.

Sash moved toward the door and freedom. She was almost there when she felt herself falling forward. She hit the cool concrete floor with a thud. Surprised by the tumble, she glanced over her shoulder to see the cause of her fall. Her captor had a hold of her ankle. A trail of blood marked his journey out of the former room and into this one.

Fury replaced panic as Sash kicked at him blindly with her free foot. He held on tightly. Spotting a round support pole near the second doorway, she grabbed it and held on but her resistance didn't stop him. Using Sash's legs for support he began to pull himself toward her.

He wasn't a big man, but he did outweigh her and as he slowly worked his way up her legs toward her torso Sash's mobility decreased. The stench of sweat and blood from his body made her nauseous as his torturous efforts to keep her prisoner brought him closer and closer to her. His breathing was labored. It came in strangled gasps. All of his strength was being spent in this last effort to win a battle that Sash was determined that he would lose.

Releasing the pole she twisted her body around as much as his weight would allow and arched her fingers into cat-like paws. Reaching down she raked her nails across his face. He howled, as his skin ripped beneath her nails. Releasing her legs, he thrashed wildly at her hand in an attempt to knock it away. Sash wiggled free and scrambled to her feet. Frightened, frenzied, and enraged beyond control, she kicked at his head, his face, and his side. Wherever he was vulnerable she kicked, until he lay on the floor, bloodied and still. Then, spent and trembling, Sash stumbled through the door and up the stairs toward the freedom she had fought for and the child who she knew waited above.

Calm replaced the frenzied fury of her encounter in the basement as she stole up the stairway. She knew that whatever she had to do she would do it when she reached the top. Carefully, she opened the wooden door just a bit, shuddering as it creaked. Peeking through the crack, she stood in the doorway listening intently, hoping that there would be no response to noise. There was none.

Cautiously, she entered the kitchen. To her right was the back exit leading to the yard and freedom. To her left was a darkened hallway and beyond was the unknown. She turned left, grabbing a butcher knife off of the kitchen counter as she did so.

Tiptoeing down the hall, she carefully opened the closed doors on each side of the hall, ready to defend herself. It wasn't necessary. Both bedrooms were empty. Clothes were tossed about haphazardly in each room—men's clothes. Working her way toward the front of the house, she found herself in the living room. It was clean, neat and unoccupied. A large picture window looked out onto the front of the house. The curtains were open.

Hurrying to the window, Sash peeked outside, using the curtains to conceal her presence. Beyond was a wide open field with trees on either side of it but nothing and no one else. Standing there in the empty house with a knife in her hand she felt lost. She had expected a confrontation, a battle between herself and the second man who had been controlling her life over the past few hours, but she wasn't prepared for this.

Running back through the house, she looked into each room again, desperately this time, rifling through closets and drawers. She raced to the back door and flung it open wildly, all caution forgotten as fear replaced desperation. The house was empty. There was no sign of her brother, no clothes, no shoes. Perhaps they had taken him outside.

She entered the backyard, standing still for a moment

listening closely for a sound, any sound that would tell her that another human being was present. There was the chirping of birds, the rustling of the wind through the trees, the distant sound of an airplane engine roaring above the trees, but no sign of her brother.

She wanted to call his name, but she might alert her captor. If the element of surprise was on her side she didn't want to loose it. Racing to the grove of trees surrounding the open field behind the house, she stood there breathlessly, waiting, listening—for the snap of a twig, the sound of a footstep. There was none.

She went as far as she could, searching the woods to no avail. Running back to the house she crossed over to the opposite grove of trees and repeated her hunt. Finding a greenhouse, she approached it with no reserve, bursting into the doorway, knife poised and ready to take a life. It was empty.

She had no idea how much time had passed when she made her way back to the house. She was near hysterics. Her brother was no where to be found. The three telephones in the house were disconnected and there was no sign of another house nearby. She needed help and she knew where she had to go to get it. That thought propelled Sash as she started to walk down the dusty road that led to the house that had been her prison. She didn't know where she was going. She had no idea where she was. Tears streamed down her cheeks as she sobbed loudly, trying in vain to calm the fear that gripped her at not having found the little boy. Fervently, she prayed that she would spot the kidnapper on the road before he spotted her, and she was hoping against hope that her brother would be with him.

As time passed and Sash continued walking, it became

evident how isolated the house had been. She had been walking for quite a while and there wasn't a soul in sight. As she trudged onward, she could feel the notebook that was tucked in her boot. Stopping, she withdrew it and scanned the pages. Her gaze settled on one single name. She needed help, desperately, and she knew where she was going to get it.

CHAPTER 1

Sash Adams. Sash Adams. Who in the world was Sash Adams? Brandon Plaine sat behind the old rolltop desk that used to belong to his father and contemplated his silent question. At age thirty-nine his memory was as sharp as a tack so he was certain that he would remember her name if he knew her. He didn't. Yet, the calls from Sash Adams had come over his private line, a line reserved for an exclusive few. Who ever this woman was, she must have gotten the telephone number from him, and it was obvious from her four frantic messages that she wanted to speak with him badly. But darn if he could remember the woman.

Of course lately his private number didn't seem to be as private anymore. He had actually gotten a crank call on the same line yesterday. It seemed that fame brought out all kinds of kooks, especially unwanted fame. Brandon glanced at the *Newsweek* magazine lying on top of his desk and gave a disgusted sigh.

The face staring back at him was almond brown, clean-shaven and square jawed. The hair was dark brown, cut close to his head, without the traces of gray he soon expected. The eyebrows were thick and perfectly arched. The eyes were dark brown and deep-set. The lips were full and the smile was noncommittal, revealing stark white teeth.

To Brandon there was nothing extraordinary about the face on the cover, but women seemed to like it. He had been told more than once that he was handsome. Some women had added the word sexy to that description, pointing out his well built six-foot three frame as evidence. Yet, he doubted that it was his looks, his intelligence or his so-called sex appeal that sparked the interest of most women. More than likely it was his money and the power it brought that attracted them, not the man. It was the image that peered back at him from the cover of *Newsweek* magazine that women were interested in. Nobody wanted to get to know the real man. The women he met were more than happy with the illusion.

Brandon read the headline beneath his name. *Plaine Dealing Plaine Style.* Even the woman writer sent to interview him had come on to him. Her professionalism had been lacking, that was for certain, but at least she had a way with words. He opened the pages of the magazine and flipped through them until he reached the article about himself. There was a black and white picture of him as a young boy with his father and another picture of him as the successful CEO sitting at his desk in his San Francisco office. There were two pictures of him posing with dignitaries and the last picture of him was out on the town with the lady of the moment. He had read the article and it was impressive. All of the articles written about him over the years had been impressive. Who would have thought that there would be so many articles? So many covers? He hadn't planned it that way. Becoming a media star had never been in the plan.

All he had ever wanted was to make his father proud of him. He had achieved that goal and gone beyond it.

His father had raised Brandon by himself and the two had been very close. When his Dad retired, Brandon's plan had been simple. He wanted to take the small family newspaper founded and operated by his father for thirty years, and expand its reach beyond the San Francisco Bay area. His goal was to diversify and to increase the voice of African-Americans in the West. Ten years ago he had gone into debt, purchased one bankrupted radio station and formed Plaine Deal Media Incorporated. Now his company was the largest minority owned multimedia conglomerate in the country.

Plaine Deal Media was at the top of *Black Enterprise* magazine's Top 100 Black companies. The corporation owned newspapers, magazines, radio and television stations nationwide. Two years ago, the company went public and mainstream media had discovered that the man behind the company's success was young, dynamic, handsome and single. Since that time, Brandon's life hadn't been the same. In the span of that short time, his face had been on the covers of *Black Enterprise*, *Ebony*, *Money* and *Entrepreneur* magazines as well as the recent *Newsweek.* Success had brought praise and recognition, but he had paid a high price for that success.

Like his father, Brandon had worked countless hours, seven days a week to make his business a success. There had been no vacations. A private life had been all but impossible. He had earned every accolade by the sweat of his brow. For over a decade, work had been all that he knew and all that he lived for, until it caught up with him.

With a flip of his wrist, Brandon closed the magazine,

got up from his desk, stood and looked out of the window. The scene before him was picture perfect. The Pacific Ocean was peaceful and serene. Clouds floated in the sky aimlessly and on the horizon a sailboat skimmed effortlessly along the water as if gliding on angel wings. He loved living on the Monterey Peninsula, despite his initial skepticism about living anywhere other than San Francisco.

It was his doctor who advised him to make the transition to the easier lifestyle on the Peninsula. His words had been simple: slow down or die. They had been offered when Brandon woke up in the hospital after collapsing in his office. Years of long hours, poor diet and little sleep had finally taken their toll.

Brandon had made the move without fanfare. That had been six months ago. He now ran his corporation from a quaint, adobe style building in Monterey, California instead of from the confines of his corporate headquarters in San Francisco. He did so with a secretary, a few computers, a fax machine and plenty of e-mails. He made a couple of appearances a month at the corporate office and discovered that he could still be effective as a CEO.

In less than a year, Brandon had changed his entire lifestyle. He now came to work in tee-shirts, shorts and sneakers instead of suits and ties. He exercised and jogged regularly and his once sparse frame was now muscular and fit. He was wealthy and healthy and in control of his world. It couldn't get better than this.

Sighing contentedly, Brandon turned from the window and flipped off his computer. It was Friday and a holiday weekend. It was time to call it quits and to feed his rumbling stomach.

* * *

Brandon's favorite restaurant, a small Mexican cantina located within walking distance of his office, was all but deserted when he entered. The restaurant was too far off the beaten path for the tourist and lunch hour was over for the locals working nearby. With a wave at Luis Torres, the restaurant owner, Brandon swung into a booth near the back.

He was digging into a healthy plate of enchiladas when he looked up to see a woman sliding into his booth, occupying the seat across from him. Surprised, Brandon sat with his fork suspended in midair, expecting to recognize her face. Quickly he searched his memory bank. The face didn't register, but what a face—sienna brown, with high, finely sculptured cheek bones, sparkling brown eyes beneath curly lashes, a beautifully shaped nose and rich, full lips. Her dark brown hair was in dreadlocks that fell past her shoulders. They were pulled away from her face into a thick, ponytail held by a rubberband. She wore no makeup but needed none. She was a very attractive woman, although presently she looked harried. Dressed in a wrinkled pair of jeans and a soiled, white sleeveless blouse, she also looked unkempt.

"May I help you?" Brandon lowered his fork, replacing his look of surprise with one of annoyance.

"You *are* Brandon Plaine, aren't you?"

"Uh, yes," Brandon replied hesitantly, noting the desperate tone in her voice. Was she seeking an autograph? His unwanted notoriety had resulted in his often being recognized and asked for his signature, but her next words told him that wasn't the case.

"Well, I'm sorry to bother you like this, Mr. Plaine, I followed you from your office building and, well..." She bit her bottom lip and swallowed as if gathering courage to continue. "I know this may sound dramatic, but what I have to say to you is a matter of life or death."

Life or death? Oh great she was a nut case. Why did he have to attract the crazies? Brandon's eyes darted toward the cash register where Luis had been standing when he entered. Maybe he could catch his eye and have him come over and remove this fruitcake, but Luis wasn't at his station. Even the waiters, who were usually so solicitous, were nowhere to be found. He and the nut case were the only two people in the dining area. Hopefully, she wasn't dangerous.

Brandon cleared his throat. "Well, I'm certain that this *is* a matter of life or death, Ms—"

"Adams. Sash Adams."

"Ms. Adams," Brandon frowned, the name sounded familiar. "But, as you can see I'm eating right now."

"I know, but..."

"And if you need to talk to me about business, you can call my administrative assistant. I'm sure she'll be happy to make an appointment for you." Brandon resumed eating, silently dismissing her, but apparently Sash Adams didn't get the message.

"I've called your office several times today."

Suddenly realizing who she was, Brandon swallowed his food so quickly that he almost choked. He coughed to clear his throat. "Oh, yes, I know who you are now. You're *that* Sash Adams. I've gotten four calls from you today."

"And you didn't answer any of them." She sounded annoyed. "Like I said, this is a matter of life or death."

Still unsure of her mental state, Brandon decided not to annoy her further. Who knew what she was capable of doing? It was better to let her have her say then maybe she would leave.

"Okay, Lady, what is so urgent that it's a matter of life or death? What is it, a record that just *has* to be played on one of my radio stations? Or do you have an article that just *has to* be printed in one of my newspapers or magazines? Just spit it out, so I can eat in peace." He resumed eating without looking up. He could feel her glaring at him.

Sash gave a shaky sigh. "No. It's nothing like that. I know that you'll be skeptical about what I'm about to say, Mr. Plaine. You'll probably think that I'm certifiably insane, but believe me so much has happened over the past few days—" Her voice wavered a bit, but she quickly regained her composure. "You see, Mr. Plaine, three days ago I was kidnapped."

"Kidnapped?" Brandon looked up from his plate and raised a disbelieving brow.

She nodded. "Yes, kidnapped. I know you don't believe me, but all I'm asking is that you hear my story before you totally dismiss me."

Increasing his guard, Brandon nodded reluctantly. He would do anything to get rid of this woman.

"Well, it all started three days ago, when Sweet and I went..."

"Sweet?"

"My brother, Trent. Sweet is his nickname. It's short for sweetheart. You see Sweet and I were in the parking lot of the Barnyard Shopping Center when...."

CHAPTER 2

"...So I hitch hiked here to Monterey to find you. You're the only one who can help me, Mr. Plaine. The only one!" Sash's voice broke. Closing her eyes momentarily she concentrated on breathing. She was determined not to shed any more tears. In the past few days she had cried enough tears.

Taking a calming breath, she opened her eyes and reined in her emotions. Brandon sat with his arms folded across his chest. The meal he had intended on eating was only half finished. He had given her his full attention as she told her story and she was grateful for that, but she needed him to believe her. He *had* to believe her. Her brother's life depended on it.

Brandon sat contemplating all that he had heard in the past half-hour. Whether the tale was that of a deranged mind or not, what she had relayed to him was riveting. Not only was she pretty, but she had quite an imagination. She had told her tale with such heartfelt emotion it almost sounded believable—*almost*.

"So you're saying that you and your brother were snatched

off a shopping center parking lot by two men in a gray cargo van..."

"Yes."

"Then you were taken to a house in Santa Cruz..."

"The Santa Cruz mountains."

"Pardon me, the Santa Cruz *mountains*, and you were kept prisoner for the past few days in this isolated spot until you escaped."

"Yes.

"Then you made your way here to me, hitchhiking all the way, mentioning none of this to anyone."

"Yes, because you're the one who they want to pay the ransom for my brother's return." Sash reached down into her boot and withdrew the small spiral bound notebook she had hidden there days ago. "I managed to sneak this notebook out of my purse when I was in the back of the van. I hid it in my boot along with the pen I told you about. I wrote everything I could down just in case something happened to us, then they wouldn't get away with it." She held the notebook out to Brandon.

"Uh huh, I see." Brandon looked at the notebook as if it were a snake about to strike. "And you say that you stabbed the kidnapper with this gold plated pen that was so lethal "

"Yes, it was a gold plated pen from Tiffany's. I tried to gouge his eye out." Sash's voice was laced with bitterness.

"Hmmm, you're a tough one aren't you?"

"I did what I had to do."

"Is that right?" Brandon couldn't hide his skepticism. "And these so called kidnappers want *me*—who has never met you or your brother in my life—to pay *them* the ransom money."

"I know it sounds strange, but..."

"*But*, the question is where is this brother of yours?"

Sash gave a shaky sigh. "It's like I told you, once I got upstairs nobody was there. I looked everywhere, all through the house, in the yard, in the woods around the house. I don't know where my brother is."

"So you just ran away and left your brother with the kidnappers."

She didn't answer as the words tore through her heart. Sash's body visibly sagged. Her reply was an agonized whisper. "Yes, I guess I did."

Brandon watched the play of emotions dance across the woman's pretty face. If her story wasn't so preposterous he would almost feel sorry for her she looked so miserable, but he was beginning to get the picture. This woman wasn't a singer or a writer. She was an actress and wanted a job.

"Well, I have to give it to you, Miss Adams…"

"Call me Sash. Everybody calls me Sash."

Brandon scoffed. "Oh, so we're getting personal now. Okay, *Sash*. I'm not going to beat around the bush. I see where you're going with this little act of yours, but I'll tell you up front, I'm only an investor in the movie business. I don't do the casting."

"What?" Sash's patience with Brandon was waning. His attitude was sarcastic and condescending. If she didn't need him for Sweet's sake…. "What are you talking about?"

"I take it that you're looking for a part in one of the movies I back."

"I told you, I'm not interested in any of that!" She had just about had it with this man. For thirty minutes she had been pouring her heart out about the most traumatic experience in her life and he thought it was a joke. "Mr. Plaine, haven't you heard a word I've said?"

She was beginning to feel that her desperate trek to Monterey to seek the help of this arrogant man might have been in vain. She opened the notebook that Brandon had pointedly ignored.

"Everything that I could see, hear or smell I wrote down in this notebook. I'm here because they kept referring to you and getting the money from you." She flipped through the notebook turning the pages rapidly. "Most of what they talked about I could only hear in snatches. They thought I was unconscious in the back of the van. There's something here about your office in Monterey. I heard them say your telephone number. See, here it is! They mentioned some other buddy of theirs or someone named Buddy, and then something about a butterfly...."

The rest of Sash's words fell on deaf ears as Brandon froze at the mention of the butterfly. A flood of memories raced through his mind. His heart slammed against his chest so violently that for a moment he wondered whether he was having a heart attack.

A butterfly. Buddy. Buddy and the butterfly. How could he ever forget?

While Sash was preoccupied with rifling through the notebook, Brandon's total concentration was directed toward appearing normal. He didn't want to give this woman a clue that any word that she uttered had an effect on him. She looked up seemingly oblivious to the momentary change in his demeanor.

"So you see, Mr. Plaine," Sash continued, "This notebook might hold the key to all this. Plus, I've got something else to show you."

Once again, Sash reached inside her pants pocket. This

time she withdrew a photograph. She placed it face down on the table.

Brandon looked at the photo then back at the woman. "What's this?"

Sash didn't answer. She watched as Brandon slowly turned the photograph over and looked at it. The shock on his face was as vivid as it had been on her own when she first saw the horrifying photograph. There, staring back at him was the nutmeg brown face of a small boy. He sat, alone, before a brick wall, looking straight into the camera. His handsome little face appeared strained and his dark brown eyes looked sad, but he seemed unaware of the gun barrel pointed at the back of his head.

Shaken, Brandon's eyes traveled from the gun barrel to the gloved hand holding the gun. A single finger rested on the gun's cocked trigger. His eyes strayed back to the boy's angelic face as his heart began to hammer in his chest.

"What kind of cruel joke is this?" His eyes stayed riveted on the boy.

"This is no joke, Mr. Plaine. This is *very* real."

Brandon could feel the tension building in his body. "Who is this? Who is this kid?"

"That's Sweet." Sash noticed the sweat that had formed on Brandon's brow. The photo seemed to be having its intended affect. Good. "That's my little brother. He's five years old."

"Your brother? Five?" Brandon's eyes shifted back to Sash. His eyes held questions that demanded answers. "Where did you get this picture?"

"They gave it to me. They said that they were going to send one like it to you."

Excited now that she had his interest Sash thrust the

open notebook toward Brandon again, pointing to a scribbled note.

"See right here. I heard them say that they would send a picture of Sweet to you and that ought to cinch the deal."

Brandon tried not to seem too eager as he took the notebook from her hand. His eyes scanned the page beyond where she was pointing, eagerly trying to verify that what he was thinking wasn't possible.

Sash probed further, trying to ascertain where matters stood with Brandon. "I take it by our conversation and the look on your face that you haven't received a picture like this or a ransom note yet?"

Half-listening, Brandon shook his head in the negative, as he flipped through the pages of the notebook. There it was again, the words Buddy and butterfly. The scribbled notes didn't confirm that the words might be related to each other, yet the coincidence....

Brandon's attention returned to the photograph. Sash pushed harder.

"I realize that this picture is shocking, Mr. Plaine, but it was necessary that I show it to you so that you can understand the gravity of this situation. I know this all seems unbelievable. It certainly is to me, but my brother's life is at stake here and I will do anything I have to do to save him."

Brandon returned his attention to the woman, still uncertain about her credibility. "Then why didn't you go to the police if you want to save your brother?"

Sash heard the continued skepticism. "I don't know where Sweet is. I don't know who has him."

"All the more reason to go to the police," Brandon interjected.

"I'm afraid that if I go to the cops the kidnappers might panic. If they panic then they might—" She choked back the words that were too frightening to utter.

"I would think that this second kidnapper you mentioned would have panicked when he came back to the house and found out that you were gone. How badly did you hurt his partner?"

"I don't know and I don't care. All I know is that you're the only link I have to them and getting my brother back and that's why I'm here."

Brandon glanced at the photo once again, studying it intently. If this was a joke it was one of the cruelest he had ever encountered. What kind of monster would use a child like this as a lark? What she was saying couldn't be possible. This photograph had to be fake.

"But I've never seen you or your brother in my life. I don't know you. Why would anyone think that I would pay a ransom for strangers?"

"From the conversation I heard it wasn't me that was being held for ransom. It was Sweet."

Brandon's heart beat quickened again. *Buddy? This kid? What was the connection?* "Why him?"

"He's a child, an innocent child, I assume that they could get more for him. Besides it's been all over the newspapers and t.v. about how you support organizations for children. You've given away a small fortune. Maybe they think you're a sucker when it comes to children."

Sucker huh? Brandon pondered her choice of words. Were they prophetic? "So you're saying that they wanted him and not you. Then why did they snatch you?"

"The man I beat up made it quite clear that the plan he and his friend had for me had nothing to do with a ransom." She looked at Brandon steadily, her expression a hardened mask. She could see that he understood the meaning behind her unspoken words.

"And when they were done with you?"

"They planned on killing me. They didn't appear to have any qualms about it. That's why I had to get away. That's why that man had to go down. It was him or me."

Brandon stifled a smile at the tough talk of a woman who stood about five feet five and couldn't have weighed more than 125 pounds. His eyes strayed back to the photo. *But there had to be a connection!* "I've never heard of anyone kidnapping somebody then demanding the ransom from a stranger."

Sash agreed. "I haven't either."

"Yeah," he grunted. "I bet."

"Mr. Plaine, if I didn't need you I wouldn't be here," snapped Sash, her annoyance at his attitude having reached its peak. "You can *believe* that! And I assure you, I am *not* in on this kidnap plot.

Brandon wasn't disturbed by the look that Sash gave him, but the photo of the gun pointed at the boy's head did disturb him. Then of course there was the word Buddy and the reference to the butterfly. Coincidence?

Turning the photo face down again, he sat back to assess Sash. Her face was pinched and anxious. There were dark circles under her eyes indicating a lack of sleep. It was obvious that something was amidst. Either she believed what she was telling him or she was a darn good actress because she had him seriously considering her story. Something was going on here. His eyes returned to the photo on the table as he used all of the instincts he had garnered as a newspaperman over the years to think this through, but nothing clicked. *Buddy*. He hadn't heard that name in years. It could be possible that the reference was to the *word* buddy, except how was the word butterfly connected? That the two were related wouldn't be common knowledge. Yet, the whole thing didn't make sense! His eyes returned to Sash.

"You know don't you, Ms. Adams, that extortion is a major crime? If you have any part in this little charade you can spend a nice little stint in jail."

It was Sash's turn to study Brandon. This was the man who was called a business genius. She had read at least one article about him and had admired his photograph. Brandon Plaine was a good-looking man and until now she thought that she would be impressed if she ever met him. She had been wrong.

"If you think that I'm a criminal, Mr. Plaine, then you can call the police. I'm sure you have a cell phone. Call them, right now. I'll sit here and wait." Sash leaned across the table within inches of Brandon's face. "But let me tell you this. If anything happens to my little brother because of you, I will hunt you down like a dog and the results won't be pretty."

Brandon didn't flinch as she looked at him steadily. She was good. Very good. He had a mind to call her bluff. Holding her eyes, he reached into his pants pocket and withdrew his cell phone. She made no effort to stop him from making the call. Brandon punched in a number and listened to it ring on the other end. He saw a flash of anger in the woman's dark, thick lashed eyes, but she made no move to escape.

Sash watched as Brandon made the call. He toyed with the edges of the picture of Sweet as he did so. She had done everything she could do to get him to believe her, but she had failed. His phone call to the police could seal Sweet's fate. She wanted to break down and cry. Only her pride kept her from doing so. It seemed that everything had gone wrong from the moment she broke free of her tormentor. Yet she lived with the hope there was one person in this world that might help her. That's why she had fought anger, fear, hunger and exhaustion to make her way to Brandon Plaine. Now, here he was within arms reach shattering her hope. It was so simple to her. If he paid the money they could get Sweet back; but she had failed to convince him of that. If anything happened to her brother, it would be her fault.

Complete despair threatened to overcome her as Sash fought to hold back the tears. It was Brandon's sharp, "Let's go" that returned her attention to him. She looked up to see him standing over her. She frowned.

"Where? Aren't we waiting here for the police?"

Brandon looked perturbed. "Did you hear me talking to the police?"

"No." Actually, she had been too lost in her own misery to pay attention to what he was doing.

"Then come on," Brandon demanded impatiently. Tossing a few bills on the table, he picked up the photo and pocketed it and the notebook. He was out of the door before it dawned on Sash that the police wouldn't be coming.

Hurriedly she slid out of the booth and exited the restaurant. She had to run to catch up with him.

"Where are we going? To the police station?" She struggled to match his long legged strides.

Brandon looked at her in exasperation. "No, we're going to my office. I didn't call the cops. I called the voice mail on my private line at the office. I got a call on that line yesterday that I thought was some sort of prank. The caller was the muffled voice of a man and he left a message that said that I would be getting the surprise of my life very soon. When I called my voice mail a few minutes ago there was a child's voice on it."

Sash stopped and grabbed Brandon's arm with enough force to catch his attention. "Was it—?" She didn't dare hope that it could be Sweet, but Brandon's nod confirmed it.

"He said that his name was Trent, and that he was five years old."

"He's alive," she gasped. "I…I wasn't sure." Closing her eyes, she gave silent thanks, then returned her attention to Brandon. "Did he say anything else?"

"Yes. He said that he needed my help."

CHAPTER 3

Sash was surprised at the simplicity of Brandon's office. She had expected lavish surroundings. Instead, the Peninsula headquarters of Plaine Deal Media consisted of five rooms located in an unassuming hacienda style building not far from downtown Monterey. The rooms were spacious but simply decorated. Brandon's office was sparsely furnished, consisting of a much used rolltop desk, an old, scarred swivel chair, a couch and two worn, leather wingbacks. Framed front pages from a newspaper named *The Caller* adorned the walls. The only photograph in the room was of a very young Brandon and an older version of himself whom she assumed was his father. It sat on his desk. The two men were dressed in fishing gear and they were holding up a large fish between them.

Sash's attention returned to Brandon. He sat with his fingers steepled under his chin in deep contemplation. He had played the voice mail message for her that contained Sweet's plaintive plea. Aware of Brandon's close scrutiny, Sash fought the tears that threatened to flow at the sound of her brother's voice. After sharing the voice mail Brandon had sat back, struck his present pose, then appeared to forget that she was in the room.

Sash wiggled impatiently in the leather office chair as Brandon continued to ignore her. He sat like a statue staring into space. Finally, she could take his silence no longer.

"Well what are we waiting for? You haven't said two words to me since we got here. I want to know what's going to be done about my brother? Are the kidnappers going to call again or what? If so, maybe we can have the call traced." She tried to keep the rising hysteria out of her voice, but was unsuccessful.

Brandon was slow in answering as his attention returned to Sash. "I don't have caller I.D. on this telephone, other than that only the authorities could trace the call and you said that you didn't want them involved. Now I have a question for you, Ms. Adams. Are you a worried sister or an extortionist? Why don't you just cut the crap and confess before this charade goes any further?"

Instantly, Sash saw red but just as quickly reason prevailed. She needed this man. Sweet needed this man. She had to keep it together. She answered calmly.

"As I've already indicated, I understand your doubts, Mr. Plaine. This all sounds so implausible, but I swear to you that every word that I've told you is true. The proof is on your voice mail."

"No." Brandon held up his finger in an effort to halt her flow of words. "What's on my voice mail is a criminal offense perpetrated by a bunch of amateurs. You see, Ms. Adams, by recording this farce you and your friends have given me enough evidence to press charges against you and put you and your playmates away for a long, long time. Not very intelligent, I assure you."

"And I assure you, Mr. Plaine that I'm quite aware of the law—local, state and federal. A law degree from Stanford University has provided me with that knowledge."

"*You're* an attorney?" Brandon looked doubtful.

"And I worked long and hard to become one. I had just gotten the news that I passed the bar exam the day Sweet and I were kidnapped. We were out celebrating. If you don't believe me, just call Stanford. They have my records. I have nothing to hide."

"Uh huh," Brandon searched her face for any hint of untruth. "And where do you live and work, since you're being so open with me? You see, as a former newspaper reporter, Ms. Adams, I'm a natural skeptic. I could call Stanford and I have no doubt that they would tell me that a Ms. Sash Adams graduated from their law school, but that doesn't mean that would be you. Anyone could obtain that information. You haven't shown me any identification. There's no proof that you're who you say you are."

"My purse and billfold were in the van."

"How convenient."

"But I live here in Monterey, on Abrego Street. I'm unemployed. I've been living on some insurance money while I studied for the bar."

"Oh, so you don't have a job. You're in need of money. Yet you said that you were carrying a gold plated writing pen. Those aren't cheap."

Sash tried to ignore the smug look on Brandon's face. "You can call my landlady, Mrs. Rosemont, she'll confirm that Sweet and I live there. As for the pen, it was a gift from a friend."

"Your *friend* does have expensive taste, doesn't she? Or is it a he? As for Mrs. Rosemont she could be in on this little scheme, too."

Sash fumed. "Mrs. Rosemont is seventy-eight years old."

"Senior citizens need money, too."

"That's it! I've had it!" Sash slammed her fist down on the top of Brandon's desk. "You may not believe anything else I've told you, but there's one thing you can believe. I wouldn't be sitting here taking your insults if I didn't have to be here! I need you to save my brother's life. He's an innocent little boy and he's out there somewhere terrified, unable to understand what's happening to him, and only God knows what *is* happening!" How could this man be so callous?

Brandon showed no reaction to her histrionics. This had to be some sort of scam and this woman was obviously part of it. All he wanted to know was how she and her partners could possibly be connected to Buddy. If not, how did they know about the butterfly? And of course there was that photograph.

Reaching into his pants pocket Brandon withdrew the photo and studied it. The entire setting with the child must have been staged. Yet, there was something about the boy. He looked from the photo to Sash. She had calmed considerably.

"Listen, Ms. Adams, this entire situation is too bizarre for me, but as busy as I am, I'm going to play along with your little game for a while."

"Play along?" Sash looked confused.

"I'm going to take you to Abrego Street, and see if you really live there."

Sash nodded in agreement. "I have no problem with that, but shouldn't we stay here? The kidnappers might call back."

Yeah, he thought so. She didn't want to go "home." Brandon rose to leave. "The boy didn't indicate when there would be another call and if a call does come in they can leave it on voice mail like before. So there's really nothing to keep us here. Is there? That is unless you have a reason for us not to go over on Abrego."

Sash rose, determined to make this man change his mind about her involvement. Pushing past Brandon she led the way to the entrance. "Come on." This time it was Brandon who followed her out of the door.

* * *

It was all too confusing for Brandon. Everything Sash had told him about herself appeared to be true. He had been on maximum alert when he and Sash arrived at the two story framed house on Abrego, which she called home. He felt fairly certain that if he ran into trouble that he could defend himself. He had earned a black belt in karate years ago. If this woman was setting a trap he was prepared. Yet, the only person he encountered at the place Sash called home was Mrs. Rosemont, her white-haired landlady who stood about five feet tall. Mrs. Rosemont had been relieved at Sash's reappearance, although she expressed concern about her disheveled appearance. She confirmed that Sash and her brother had been inexplicably absent for a couple of days and she had been worried about them. Sash apologized for worrying her then informed the older woman that she and her brother had taken an unexpected trip to see a friend in the Bay Area. She told her that Sweet was staying with them for a while.

Mrs. Rosemont appeared to accept the explanation before

turning her attention to Brandon. Sash introduced him as a friend then dismissed further questioning by explaining to her landlady that she had lost the key to her second floor apartment. After Mrs. Rosemont provided her with a spare key Sash hustled Brandon outside.

The second floor apartment had to be accessed from an exterior stairway located on the side of the house. The apartment Brandon entered was spacious with plenty of bay windows that allowed an abundance of sunshine to stream into its neat interior. The living and dining rooms were furnished in solid, comfortable furniture that appeared to be well maintained. Everything in the room had an African motif, from the colorful printed curtains at the window, to the mud cloth area rug covering the polished wood floors. African masks and finely weaved baskets decorated the walls, interspersed with framed prints by African-American artists. There were plants everywhere, hanging from the ceilings and trailing from planters on windowsills. There were two giant potted palm trees in the living room, and an elephant ear plant almost as large as an elephant in the dining room. All of the plants appeared to be healthy and thriving. It seemed that Sash Adams had a green thumb.

Brandon noted the numerous family photographs scattered throughout the rooms. Most were of Sweet at various ages. He picked up one picture of the boy seated between a handsome middle-aged couple. The three of them looked into the camera with wide, happy smiles.

Responding to the look of curiosity on Brandon's face as he examined the picture. Sash walked over to him and took the picture from his hand. She smiled down at it sadly. "Those are our parents, Mildred and James Curry."

"Curry?" Brandon raised a questioning brow.

"My brother's last name is Curry," Sash explained. "James Curry was my stepfather."

"*Was* your stepfather?"

Lovingly, Sash placed the picture frame back on the table. "Our parents were killed in an accident two years ago. It's just Sweet and me now."

There was a moment of silence as Brandon struggled for something to say. *I'm sorry* seemed shallow, and he still wasn't sure that he believed all that this woman was telling him. This could be another sob story.

Sash broke the silence. "Follow me, I'll show you Sweet's room."

Still cautious of his surroundings, Brandon followed Sash down a short hallway, past a closed door—which he assumed was Sash's room. They passed a bathroom strikingly decorated in zebra stripes, then stopped at a second closed door that Sash opened for Brandon. He stepped past her and over the threshold.

The boy's walls were painted sky blue. Large, fluffy clouds made of cotton balls hung from the ceiling, suspended from thin, nearly invisible wires. A bright yellow sun, wearing black sunglasses and a toothpaste smile was painted on one wall, talking trees, dancing bears and flowers were painted on another wall. A colorful rug covered the polished wood floor.

Another wall contained a built-in bookshelf filled with books. Beneath it stood a wicker chest that served as a toy box. Except for a pair of small sneakers tossed haphazardly on the floor next to the twin bed, the room was neat and spotless. A lot of care and love had gone into creating this child space.

"Did you decorate this room?"

Sash nodded.

"And the murals?"

"I painted them."

"You're very talented."

She shrugged. "Thank you. Art is my hobby."

Fighting the emotions that erupted at the sight of Sweet's empty room, Sash cleared her throat and pushed away from the doorway. "If you don't mind, I'm barely standing on my feet. I'm going to grab a quick shower to keep me awake, slip into something clean and then we can talk about coming up with a plan to get my brother back."

Sash stepped away from the doorway indicating that the tour was over. Brandon conceded, closing the bedroom door behind him. He followed her down the hall. She stopped at the first closed door that they had passed.

"What's in that room?" Brandon nodded toward the closed door behind her.

"My bedroom."

"Let me see." It was an order not a request.

Defiant, Sash started to block his entrance, but then relented. She was too tired to fight with this man. She opened the door and Brandon stepped into Sash's bedroom

The room's décor held Sash's decorative touch. Like the other rooms the décor was African. The drapes, bedspread and the skirt to Sash's dressing table were all made out of the same zebra print material as the shower and window curtains in the bathroom. Murals of exotic plants and animals were painted on one wall. As in the other rooms, well-maintained plants were placed about. A picture of her parents was strategically placed on the nightstand next to her bed. A similar picture had been in Sweet's room as well.

"Satisfied?" Sash's voice was tight. As necessary as it might have been she still didn't like Brandon playing inspector in her home.

Brandon nodded and stepped back into the hallway.

"Well I'm glad I passed inspection." It was Sash's turn to be sarcastic. "Now if you don't mind I'm going to take my shower. It won't take long. Make yourself at home. There's some bottled water and some juice in the refrigerator." Without further ceremony she closed the door in his face.

Brandon returned to the living room his curiosity having increased even more about this defiant woman with the eclectic sense of style. Who was Sash Adams really? She had stepped into his life out of nowhere two and a half-hours ago with this fantastic story of hers and he could feel himself being pulled into her world. What was he doing here? The woman might be a criminal. But what kind of criminal takes you to her home and gives you a tour? Could the little old landlady be involved in this? Mrs. Rosemont seemed sincere. Of course that could all be part of the act. If so, he had to give them credit. They had planned this little caper with great care. Still, he didn't trust this woman. On the way to her home she had questioned him as to whether anything in the notebook held any meaning for him. He had been noncommittal. He chose to give away nothing until he found out what was going on.

Settling on the couch, Brandon sat back to think this situation through. In the background he could hear the sound of the running water coming from the bathroom where Sash was bathing. For an instant a fleeting image of her shapely figure flashed before his eyes. Shaking the image from his mind, Brandon brought his attention back to the matter at hand. He didn't need to get distracted by a pretty face and a few well placed curves. He had to get down to business.

Taking the notebook from his jacket pocket, he leafed through it.

The notebook contained random, scribbled notes that substantiated much of what Sash had told him. The word Buddy was written twice. She hadn't capitalized it, not knowing if it was a description or a name. The word butterfly was scribbled only once, with no accompanying note to explain its meaning. Other than that she had written no substantial information as to how those words he recognized fit into the entire picture. Maybe the word buddy *was* a description and not a formal name. Maybe the butterfly reference wasn't as relevant as he thought. Maybe this whole thing was an elaborate joke. But who would pull such a cruel joke? It all seemed too unbelievable to be true. This had to be some sort of scheme!

Closing the notebook, Brandon got up and roamed the room looking for any sign that this apartment wasn't what it appeared to be. In his search he stumbled across several photo albums.

An hour later he had looked through all of the albums. They had chronicled the life of a woman who from all indications came from a happy, middle class family and who had accomplished a lot in her life. Sash Adams had excelled in both academics and in sports. She had been a cheerleader, a prom queen and had graduated from college Phi Beta Kappa. There were photos that showed that she had traveled extensively throughout Europe and the Caribbean. One entire album was filled with a pictorial chronicle of her having lived for a while in West Africa; but it was the pictures near the end of the album that brought Brandon the biggest surprise.

In several different poses that went from a friendly side-by-side pose to an intimate kiss caught on film, Sash was in the photos with a man—a tall, slender African whose dress fluctuated from traditional African attire to expensive, tailored suits. From the looks on each of their faces in the photos, a romantic relationship evolved—a relationship that resulted in an engagement ring. In one photo Sash was all smiles as she stood wrapped in the man's arms while she flashed a large diamond ring at the camera. *An engagement ring? He didn't remember seeing any engagement ring on her finger.* Brandon's eyes moved from Sash's happy face to that of the man whose arms in which she was wrapped. From the look on his face as he gazed at her, this was a man deeply in love. This also was a man with whom Brandon was familiar. His eyes fell to the writing below the picture to confirm what he already knew. It read: Michael and me at the LaFoe party. *Michael. Michael Ramuba.* Sash Adams had been engaged to Michael Ramuba, a member of one of the wealthiest families in West Africa. That could explain the expensive pen she had described to him.

Brandon knew Michael. They had conducted business transactions over the years, but neither had ever discussed their private lives with the other. Brandon's eyes strayed to the day and date written beneath the photo. It had been taken two years ago, on Valentine's Day. Brandon closed the album, his brows drawn in concentration. Finally, here was proof of a connection between someone he knew and the mysterious Sash Adams. Yet, the discovery only deepened the mystery, not solved it. Was it just a coincidence that they both happened to know Michael? What were the chances of that happening?

He was sure that Michael wasn't involved in any kind of plot. Money was no object for him. Then why would someone like Sash, who was ready to marry into money, be involved in one? If she needed money why didn't she go to Michael for it? None of this made sense. He had to have some answers.

Laying the last album aside, Brandon withdrew his cell phone and dialed a number. A deep male voice answered on the second ring.

"John Nathan."

"John, I've got a job for you and your security team. I need some information and I need it like an hour ago." Filling him in on the details, Brandon disconnected, feeling more in control since Sash Adams had made herself at home at his dining table.

Glancing at his watch Brandon was surprised to see the amount of time that had passed since he and Sash entered her apartment. The silence in the apartment indicated that she had finished her shower, but she hadn't emerged from the bedroom. Deciding to hurry her along, he rose and walked down the hallway to her bedroom, determined to get some of the answers to the additional questions he had.

One of those questions concerned the child, Sweet. Where was he really? Several of the photo albums confirmed that there was a child in her life. There were no pictures of the boy as a baby, but from the time that he was a toddler there seemed to be someone there with a camera to take photos of his every move. Every picture in the albums had a neatly scripted explanation of where and when it was taken. From what Brandon could discern Sweet must have been a change of life baby for his parents. Sash was at least twenty-nine or thirty years old when her brother was born. That would make her around thirty-four or thirty-five.

Brandon stood outside the closed door and gently tapped. "Ms. Adams?" There was no response.

After a second knock and the same lack of response, Brandon opened the door cautiously and peeked inside. Sash lay on her bed asleep. Brandon stepped inside the bedroom and instantly regretted his decision.

Exhaustion had claimed Sash before she'd gotten the opportunity to dress. A lacy bra and matching bikini panties lay at the foot of the bed. Sash lay spread eagle on the bed with only an oversized towel covering her body. The towel threatened to reveal more than she intended. Brandon felt a tug at his midsection as he approached the bed.

Sash looked different lying there sleeping. She looked peaceful. The pinched lines of worry and exhaustion were missing from her face. Her dark brown tresses, no longer in a ponytail cascaded loosely pass her shoulders framing her attractive face. This was a good-looking woman, from her head to her toes. Brandon reached for a thin cotton blanket neatly folded on a nearby chair and covered her tempting torso. That helped his rising libido a little. A brief glimpse at her left hand, before covering her, had confirmed that there was no engagement ring on her finger. Unconsciously, Brandon's lips curved into a satisfied smile.

Going to the bay window, he closed the vertical blinds. The room darkened. Standing at the window, Brandon glanced back at the sleeping Sash. She hadn't moved a muscle since he entered the room. Some extortionist! He decided to let her sleep. He'd get the answers to the questions later. Meanwhile, he would continue to search the apartment.

He was headed for the door when the telephone on her wicker bedstand rang. Brandon froze as his eyes darted to

Sash who continued to sleep undisturbed. On the third ring the answering machine by her bed answered the call. A recorded message asked for the caller to leave their name and number. On the other end a muffled, masculine voice complied.

Sash Adams we know that you're in your apartment and we know who's with you. We'd advise you to answer this telephone call now. If you don't, you'll be responsible for a sacrifice we're sure you don't want to make. You have ten seconds to answer.

The caller fell silent. With his heart pounding furiously, Brandon moved swiftly across the room and shook Sash, calling her name as he made his way to the telephone. Everything in him told Brandon that the sudden appearance of Sash Adams was about to change his life forever.

CHAPTER 4

In the distance Sash could hear Sweet call her name. He had to be here somewhere. She had been looking desperately for hours, racing through the thickening fog engulfing the dense forest, calling his name, but there had been no answer, until now. The sound of his voice brought renewed determination. She stood still and alert, hardly breathing—waiting.

"Sash!"

There it was. Sweet was calling her name!

"Wake up! Now!"

Sash awakened with a jolt to find herself sitting in her bed being shaken like a rag doll. She tried to clear the cobwebs from her mind. "W..what? What the…"

"Answer the telephone. It's them!"

A man's harsh voice reached her subconscious. Who was he? What was he doing here? Where was…?

"Sweet!"

Instantly, Sash snapped to attention. She didn't have to ask to whom the voice belonged. With a silencing finger to his lips, Brandon pointed to the telephone then pressed the speakerphone button so that he could listen to the conversation. Still groggy from sleep her voice was husky from exhaustion.

"Hello?"

The voice on the other end was deliberately distorted, and it sounded angry. "What kind of games are you playing, lady? Do you want to see this kid again or not?"

"You give my brother back to me and he'd better be alive!"

"What part of this deal don't you understand? You don't give the orders, we do. That escape stunt of yours is going to cost you. Put Plaine on the line."

She looked at Brandon, surprised that the caller knew that he was there with her. Brandon didn't appear to be disturbed by the revelation.

"I'm here. What do you want?"

"One million dollars in unmarked bills. I want them delivered in two plain shopping bags. We'll let you know where and when at 9:00 tomorrow morning. You'll be contacted at your office."

"What makes you think that I'm going to pay a million dollars for a kid who I don't know?"

"You'll pay."

"Oh yeah? Tell me why?"

"A little butterfly on my shoulder tells me that you will. Know what I mean?"

"No." Brandon managed to keep his voice steady as he lied.

The laughter on the other end was guttural "Think about it hard, *buddy.*"

Brandon didn't bite. "So we're playing riddles instead of abduction?"

"Like I told the woman, this is no game. Give us the money or the kid will die. And remember, no cops."

"How do you know we haven't already called the authorities? "

"You haven't. We've been watching you. If you had, the woman would be looking for a body. Remember, 9:00 a.m. tomorrow at your office." The call was disconnected.

Sash's eyes widened. "There it is, the word butterfly! Just like I wrote. What's this butterfly thing about?"

Brandon didn't answer. Sash reached for the floor lamp by her bed and turned on the light. The glow softened the room's shadows as it settled on Brandon's face. He was studying her thoughtfully, "I was wondering, Ms. Adams, why would this so called kidnapper be watching us?"

"I was wondering the same thing and don't call me Ms. Adams. You know my first name." Sash sprang to her feet only to be reminded that she was dressed in a towel. Gripping the top of the towel tightly, she tried to ignore her self-consciousness. "I have no idea how he knows anything, but he does seem to know a little something about you. Why is that?"

Brandon's eyes traveled from Sash's well-shaped legs up to the cleavage teasing him beneath the towel. She was astute as well as beautiful. That could be a deadly combination. Unsettled, he moved across the room and sat in a rocking chair.

"My guess is that predators study their victims. But I'm not the subject here. I was thinking that maybe this guy is watching us because he doesn't trust you." Brandon crossed his arms triumphantly. From the stricken look on Sash's face he had not only successfully avoided her inquiry about him, but he had put her back on the defensive.

Across the room Sash eyed Brandon skeptically, noting his primal appraisal of her. Grabbing her terry cloth robe from the foot of her bed, she slipped it on over the towel and tied the sash securely. Feeling more in control, she approached him.

"*Your* theory is preposterous, *Mr. Plaine*, but I've got another one. Maybe this is some sort of media stunt and you and some friends of *yours* are playing some kind of sick joke that got out of hand, like for that show that's on one of your television stations. What's the name of it? *Where's the Camera* or whatever it's called."

Brandon snorted. "You have got to be kidding!"

"No I'm not. I've been wondering myself why a kidnapper would pick a stranger to pay the ransom. It makes no sense."

"I already said that."

"So maybe it's some sort of publicity stunt engineered by you and your staff."

"Lady, I need publicity like I need a hole in the head."

Wearily, Sash sat on the side of her bed. That was true. She sighed, knowing that she had been grasping at straws. "Okay. This bickering is getting us nowhere. We've got to be rational."

Brandon weighed her words and those of the abductors. How in the world would anyone know about the butterfly? Maybe it was crazy, but he was beginning to believe that this thing might be for real. "You're right. We do need to be rational."

Rising, he walked over to the closed blinds and peeked through the slits to the street below. As he suspected, there was no one to be seen. The street was empty of pedestrians. Cars were parked along the street, but from what he could see they appeared empty.

Sash was frightened. They were being watched. The man

watching them knew about her having escaped and about her attack on his partner. He said that she would pay. Had the caller taken his revenge out on Sweet? There were a million questions tumbling through her mind, but presently only one question was paramount. "Are you going to pay the ransom?"

Brandon turned from the window in time to see the look on Sash's face. It showed fear, vulnerability. This was a new look for her. In the short time that he had known her he had seen looks of uncertainty, defiance and anger, but this look was different. It was a look that he didn't want to affect him. He still harbored a shadow of doubt about her involvement. Yet, still there was—

Brandon reclaimed his seat. "Sash, what's your relationship with Michael Ramuba?"

The question took Sash completely by surprise. "You know Michael?" Springing from the bed she marched across the room to stand in front of Brandon. "How do you know Michael? If this is one of his tricks to get me back it's sick!"

Brandon rose in one swift movement, nearly chest to chest with Sash. She looked as if she was ready to fight.

"Don't get excited. I saw some pictures of you two in your photo albums in the other room."

"My photo albums? You've been going through my things?" Sash's temperature escalated.

"Hold on, Ms. Adams...Sash. You came to me wanting a small fortune to save your brother and now you're telling me that I don't have the right to find out something about you. Excuse me, but I've got a problem with that."

His words stifled Sash's anger. "That doesn't mean that I have to like your snooping." Tense, she settled back on the bed. Brandon returned to his seat.

Sash was still unnerved by the coincidence of his knowing Michael. "Okay, so explain to me how you know Michael."

"We've done business together and according to what I saw in your album, you and he are engaged."

"We *were* engaged."

Brandon couldn't help but smile at the swiftness with which she corrected his error. "Fine, *were* engaged. From what I've gathered by your reaction you're not above suspecting that he might be involved in this kidnapping. Am I right?"

"Of course not!" Sash denied. *Could it be possible?* "If you know him like you say you do then you know that he wouldn't do something like this."

"I don't know Ramuba outside of our business dealings. It was you who made it sound like you think that he's capable of pulling a stunt like this for revenge."

"No, I don't think that he is." She could hear the doubt in her voice. She amended the statement. "No, never. He was hurt and angry by our breakup, but he wouldn't do something like this to me, and Lord knows he doesn't need the money." Sash rose and stood over Brandon. "Anyway, what has my relationship with Michael got to do with all of this? Do you want me to go to him for the money instead of you? Is that it?"

"I didn't say that."

"Well believe me, if it takes that to save my brother's life, I'll do it." With that Sash stormed out of the room slamming the door behind her. A second later she came back into the room, angrier than when she left. She pointed Brandon toward the door. "This is *my* bedroom. *You* get out!"

Brandon left, slamming the door behind him to emphasize his displeasure with her behavior. Her anger was irrational and so was she.

Sash searched her dresser drawers looking for something to wear. Enough was enough! Over the past few days she had been through hell and she wasn't about to go through more hell with the arrogant Mr. Plaine. Yes, she needed him for Sweet's sake, but if she had to find her baby brother by herself, she was ready and willing to do it. Putting on her underwear and snatching a tee-shirt and a pair of jeans from the drawer, she pulled the wrinkled clothing on haphazardly as her anger rapidly turned to despondency. She didn't care how she looked. What did it matter anyway? Because of some childish temper tantrum she may have cost her brother his life. She had made a major mistake.

Brandon Plaine was the best chance she had to save Sweet's life and she had just alienated him, even worse, tossed him out of her house. What if the kidnapper saw him leave and concluded that he wasn't going to pay the ransom? Suppose Brandon called the police? Maybe she could catch him. If she had to she would swallow her pride and beg him to forgive her.

Grabbing the house key, Sash hurried to the door and rushed into the hallway, bumping straight into a solid wall of chest. Strong arms reached out to stop her from toppling to the floor as Brandon steadied her. For a moment they stood staring at each other as he continued holding her. Each looked at the other expectantly, knowing that their fates were cast. Brandon was the first to break the silence, as he gave a sigh of resignation. "So we know that they're watching us. Now we have to figure out what we're going to do next."

CHAPTER 5

"Do you see them?" Sash glanced at the rear view mirror on the passenger side. "I don't see anything. What about you?" She was nervous and on edge.

"Just relax. If they follow us, they follow us." Brandon's manner was matter-of-fact.

Brandon's outward calm was getting on Sash's nerves. Didn't anything rattle this man? He was used to being in charge and that's exactly what he did. He took charge. Her opinion appeared to be of no concern.

Brandon had called his bank in San Francisco and easily acquired a bank draft for the needed money. He asked that it be deposited in an account in a bank in Monterey. They were now on their way there to get the money. Sash had provided two large shopping bags from her place in which to put the funds. She looked down at them tucked snugly at her feet hoping that they could accommodate such a large amount. Brandon had brought a briefcase along, saying that it would look odd if he used the bags to transport the money from the bank. She had to admit that he had a point, but she wondered if such a large amount would fit in what he brought.

Satisfied with the progress of their unusual expedition so far, Sash glanced at the dashboard clock. It was 5:50. Brandon was driving as if he had no place to go.

"How far is your bank? Is it much further?"

"It's about fifteen minutes away."

"What! Do you see the time? Banks close at 6:00 on Fridays and they won't be open tomorrow because of the holiday. Don't you think you ought to speed it up a bit?"

Annoyed, Brandon sighed. So the woman was a backseat driver on top of everything else! "Okay, you want speed. I'll give you speed."

Brandon's foot went down on the accelerator as they raced along the highway at warp speed. His finely tuned Mercedes sports car was rocking and rolling near 85 M.P.H. and Sash was holding onto the dashboard for her life waiting to hear the sound of a siren at any time interrupt their flight into the stratosphere.

They pulled into the bank parking lot at 5:58. The building was dark and the parking lot was empty.

Looking baffled, Sash turned to Brandon. "What's going on? It looks like it's closed!" She stared at the building fighting her rising fear. "I thought banks stayed open late on Friday. " She glanced at the clock again, reassuring herself that they still had their precious two minutes.

Brandon studied the building through the windshield. "You're right. It should be open." Climbing out of the car, he walked briskly to the front door and was greeted by a handwritten sign taped to the door.

IN MEMORY OF OUR COWORKER, MARGE SMITH, THIS BRANCH WILL CLOSE EARLY ON FRIDAY SO THAT CO-WORKERS MAY ATTEND HER FUNERAL. WE APOLOGIZE FOR THE INCONVENIENCE TO CUSTOMERS.

The branch manager had signed it. Brandon knocked on the glass in the door. There was no response. He peered beyond the sign into the semi-darkness of the deserted building as if wanting to confirm the obvious. He saw nothing. The bank was closed.

As he walked back to the car he saw Sash, standing with her body placed between the car and the opened door, watching him with anxious eyes.

"It's not open is it?"

He shook his head. "Funeral." He slid back into the vehicle without further explanation. Sash followed.

"What are we going to do now?" Her tone was a frightened whisper.

He could feel her fear and it bothered him. He preferred it when she was hopeful.

At her apartment he had started to leave in a huff when she had so unceremoniously tossed him out of her bedroom. After all, it was *she* who needed him, not vice versa. He had almost made it to her front door when he made the mistake of jamming his hands into his pockets and felt the photo he had retrieved from the table in the restaurant. It only took one look at the face of little Trent Curry and he knew that he would never forgive himself if something really did happen to the child. He made up his mind then and there to see this through to some sort of conclusion. If nothing else, the whole thing could make a good news story.

Right now it was beginning to look like a good movie script. Using his car phone, he started punching in numbers. Sash looked alarmed.

"Who are you calling?"

"The bank. The telephone number is on the door."

Sash glanced at the tomb-like building then back at Brandon. "But you said it was closed."

"The San Francisco bank called and told them I was coming. Somebody should be inside waiting for me."

Sash knew that Brandon's smug demeanor was meant to impress her. He was well aware of his influence. A mere heartbeat passed when she heard...

"Hello, this is Brandon Plaine. I'm outside in the parking lot waiting to be let in."

His manner was authoritarian, meant to initiate immediate action. A moment later a suit clad bank employee appeared at the front door.

"Well, excuse me for ever doubting you." said Sash, flashing him a smile, relieved at his having garnered positive results.

Brandon's heart skipped a beat as he glimpsed at Sash. This was the first time he'd seen her smile since they had met earlier that day. It was effervescent; but, the moment of good feelings was short-lived.

"Come on, let's go." Reaching back, he grabbed the briefcase and started to get out of the car. Her next words stopped him.

"I'm not going in."

Brandon's eyes were wary. "Why not?" *Maybe she was making sure that she wouldn't be identified later.*

"I can't go inside looking like this." Sash indicated her haphazard dress. "How would you explain *me.*"

Brandon relaxed his stance. "I don't have to explain anything." His eyes swept her wrinkled clothing. "But, all right." Exiting the car, he turned back to her before proceeding. "How do you know that I won't tell the branch manager what the money is for?"

As she looked at him, Sash's eyes were filled with all of the hope that she had put in this man. "I don't." Brandon didn't reply as she watched him walk away.

He was her hope. He was all that she had right now, and as she sat in his car in that empty parking lot she prayed as fervently as she had in that dank basement days ago. She prayed that everything would be all right. God hadn't abandoned her and he hadn't abandoned Sweet. Surely, she wouldn't have gotten this far for things not to turn out right.

The minutes seemed to tick by slowly as Sash sat and waited. The bank was a single building structure nestled against a backdrop of forest greenery. It resembled an upper middle class home rather than a business establishment, and fit in well with the other commercial edifices surrounding it. She noticed several expensive looking boutiques, an upscale coffee shop and a fancy gourmet grocery store that reminded her of how long it had been since she had eaten. Yet, she ignored the nagging hunger pains and the fatigue that threatened to overcome her and kept watch. Every sound had her jumping nervously. Each car that passed had her peering inside to see if anyone of them could contain Sweet's elusive abductors, keeping watch. When she heard the distant sound of a siren, Sash held her breath as she waited to see if it was the authorities coming to arrest her. It was clear that Brandon still didn't trust her, so she didn't release that breath until she saw him come out of the bank.

She watched him through the windshield, his long-legged gait, slow, smooth and self-assured. Dressed in his casual attire, he looked like any of the locals who had just conducted business at their local bank. He appeared calm, composed. No one would suspect that he was carrying one million dollars in the nondescript briefcase in his hand. It had taken him exactly fifteen minutes to pick it up.

Opening the car door, Brandon tossed the briefcase onto the backseat and slid gracefully into the car. Sash leaned toward him to take a peek over her shoulder at the bundle he had so carelessly tossed aside. She stopped within inches of Brandon, so close that he could smell the scent of the perfumed soap with which she had showered. The fragrance had been teasing his senses for over an hour. He inhaled. He liked it.

"That's a million dollars in there?" Sash's voice was filled with awe.

"Yep." Starting the car, he pulled out of the lot and onto the street. "I wasn't told what denominations to get so I asked for hundred dollar bills."

Sash calculated the figures in her head. "That's ten thousand one hundred dollar bills." She looked back at the case again. "One million dollars in *that.*" She returned her attention to her nonchalant savior. "It must be nice."

"To do what? Go in and get my own money? As I'm sure you're well aware, I have millions of dollars in the bank, and I worked hard for every dime. Nobody gave it to me, and I value every cent..."

"Brandon..."

"And for someone to think that they can force their way into my life and take what I've earned and believe that I'm going to lay down and take it..."

"Brandon..."

"Well, they can think again, because I'm not one to..."

"Brandon! Let it go!"

Brandon was startled out of his angry tirade by Sash's sharp command. "What do you mean 'let it go'? Here I am getting the money to save your brother and you tell me to let it go?"

"It's over and done. You've got the money. So, let's channel our energy in a new direction—delivering it so I can get Sweet back."

Brandon rolled his eyes skyward. *Channel our energy?* What kind of psycho-babble was that? He opened his mouth to protest and found that he had no defense against her reasoning. The woman made sense. Why waste energy on a task that was already completed?

He stole a glance at Sash who lay with her head resting against the car's leather headrest. He liked a woman who didn't let emotion dictate her reasoning, and right now it was reasoning that was needed.

Behind closed lids, Sash felt both the jerk of the car and the tension radiating from Brandon. She knew that this situation angered him, as it did her, but this was the most emotional outburst she had witnessed from him. She sensed that he held tight control over his emotions and that this display was unusual for him. It would have been interesting to delve into his personality further, but right now she didn't have the energy. Her head was throbbing. Her stomach was churning and she was physically and mentally exhausted. She hadn't meant to go to sleep at her apartment, precious time had been wasted, but the short rest helped to clear her mind. Now all she needed was to think clearly enough to get through tomorrow when they dropped the ransom money, then Sweet would be home.

Yet, Sash was sure that because of Brandon's suspicions about her part in the kidnapping he could still change his mind about the money. He had it, but he didn't have to deliver it. He could be merely stringing her along. It seemed that every time she looked up he was scrutinizing her. She had been shocked that he hadn't turned her into the police at the restaurant. She hadn't forgotten his earlier threat to do so and his outburst further demonstrated his deep resentment at being thrust into his present position. Despite what he thought of her, she was beginning to like Brandon Plaine. He had the ability to think quickly on his feet and she liked that about him. What she didn't like was his bossy attitude, but for now she had to live with it. After all, she didn't have much of a choice.

Yawning, Sash sank deeper into the plush leather seat of the Mercedes Benz. Brandon might not trust her but she had to trust him. Turning, she was about to say something to him, but instead of her mouth opening her head fell to her chest involuntarily and she sank into slumber, her troubles momentarily forgotten.

CHAPTER 6

Angrily, Brandon threw the cordless telephone across the room where it landed on the Italian leather sofa facing the fireplace. This couldn't be happening to him! He had influence and power, yet he couldn't reach one single person who could help him with the matter at hand. He had called the CEO of his bank to inform him of his financial need. The man couldn't be reached. Brandon had then tried to track down the CFO of his own company. Again, he was unsuccessful. The same held true when he tried to contact the CEO of the firm that oversaw his investments. It seemed that everyone had taken this particular weekend to go away and leave no way to be reached. He thought he had the answer to his predicament earlier after he called John Nathan to tell him of the latest development in his intriguing adventure with the mysterious Ms. Adams.

"The kidnappers called again," Brandon informed John.

"Where? At the office?" John asked on the other end.

"No, right here in my own home."

"At your house!"

"Yes, about twenty minutes ago."

"Damn!"

"My sentiments exactly."

Brandon had decided not to take a sleeping Sash back to her apartment since it was being watched. Instead, he took her to his house that was located in an exclusive, gated community, protected by guards and security patrols. He figured that there he could watch her. If she were involved in this illicit affair she would be physically separated from her fellow criminals.

Sash didn't stir as he carried her upstairs and placed her in the middle of his bed. Taking her shoes off, he placed them beside the bed and covered her with a blanket. Fleetingly, Brandon wondered why he chose his own bedroom suite in which to place her rather than one of the many other rooms in his spacious home. However, shrugging the thought aside, he had just settled in his downstairs office with the woman asleep upstairs lingering heavily on his mind when the telephone rang. He picked up on the second ring.

"Plaine."

"I see you can follow orders, but you need to be taught a lesson."

Brandon was stunned. He now was being contacted in his own home. They knew where he lived. They had his home number! When all of this was over everybody involved was going down! Hard! The voice continued.

"I don't appreciate you and that sneaky slut trying to outrun me today."

They had been followed to the bank and to his home.

"It's going to cost you."

Brandon was enraged. "Cost me? I would think that one million dollars is cost enough."

"You're wrong. It's two million dollars now. Payment for that little stunt that you pulled."

"You're crazy! I haven't got enough time to get the extra million."

"Two million dollars, tomorrow. I'll call your office at nine a.m. sharp." The line went dead.

"I want this to stop, John." Brandon's voice was steel as he repeated the kidnapper's demand. "I called the guards at the gate and they said that they didn't see any suspicious cars in the area. Yet, they followed us to the bank and then here. I thought your men were tailing us! Where are they? Why didn't they spot them?"

John made no excuses for the breach in security. He apologized, but he did offer a theory as to how the kidnappers got his home number. "Maybe the woman called and told them."

Instantly, Brandon rejected that possibility. "She's been asleep since we got here. There's no way she could have done that between the time I put her to bed and I came downstairs and got the call. You just get on tightening the security around us without her knowing it. Meanwhile, I'll see about getting the additional money."

"Are you ready to bring in the authorities yet?" John had urged that they be contacted from the very beginning.

Brandon hesitated. He had wanted to avoid the inevitable a while longer, certain that his own security people could handle these amateurs. Perhaps he had been wrong.

"No." He swallowed, hoping that he wouldn't regret his decision. "Let's see what happens. Just make sure your men stay closer to us."

Brandon had made his follow-up calls after talking with

John. Unfortunately, each one proved fruitless. Coming up with that much money on such short notice was proving difficult. It was 7:00 p.m.; he had fourteen hours to gather an extra million on a holiday weekend. Improbable, but not impossible. It was time to initiate another plan.

Tucked away deep in the recess of a small coat closet in his office was a hidden safe. Tossing aside the official papers and forms that seemed to dominate his life, he withdrew two stacks of rubber banded bills. He didn't have to count them. He knew that there was only $12,500 in each stack, $25,000 all together—far from what he needed. A blind person could look at the stacks of bills and see that. But could they look into a couple of shopping bags and recognize two million dollars in one glance? He doubted it. What he needed was enough cash to foster the illusion that there was that much money in those sacks.

Brandon reviewed his options. He kept a few hundred dollars in the safe at his Monterey office. Then there was a safe at his San Francisco office, that could yield him another twenty-five to thirty thousand dollars, but that was it. All he could get his hands on in the next few hours was a little over fifty thousand cash. It might not look like enough to secure the boy's release.

As he tucked all of the money into his briefcase—which he would eventually transfer to the shopping bags Sash had provided—Brandon chuckled to himself. He remembered a time when getting his hands on just the fifty thousand dollars would have had him turning cartwheels; but right now the bundles of bills clustered together looked like a mere pittance. How times had changed.

* * *

Groggily, Sash awakened. Yawning, she stretched leisurely. Adjusting to the darkness around her, she lay listening for the familiar sounds in her apartment—the drip of the sink in the bathroom, the brush of leaves against the living room window. She listened closely, but heard nothing but silence. She propped herself up on her elbows. Where were her sounds?

Reaching out to turn on the floor lamp by her bed she discovered that it wasn't there. Where was she? The last thing she remembered was being in Brandon's car.

Scrambling to her knees, Sash felt around on the nightstand next to the bed until her hand came in contact with a series of buttons built into the nightstand. Recessed lights in the ceiling above the bed beamed down on her. The lights were dim. Fumbling with the buttons, she increased their brightness until the room was flooded with light. Looking around her it became clear that nothing in this room belonged to her. It had to belong to someone else, and that someone was Brandon Plaine.

It also became clear that despite his last name there was nothing plain about Brandon's taste. It was very contemporary and it was very expensive. The room she occupied was a testimony to that.

The room was huge, larger than Sash's entire apartment and everything in it indicated the wealth of its usual occupant. The floors were mahogany inlaid with intricate geometric patterns that added to its beauty. The bed that Sash had been sleeping on was an oversized, Danish modern platform bed also made of mahogany, with matching nightstands. One wall of the bedroom consisted of floor-to-ceiling windows. Opposite the wall of windows was a large sitting area dominated by an ultra modern fireplace with pillows scattered before it. A built-in entertainment center took up the wall near the fireplace. The entire setting resembled a bachelor's studio apartment rather than a bedroom. She had read that Brandon was popular with the ladies. She could only imagine how many women he had "entertained" in this room.

As she left the bedroom, Sash didn't want to question why she was so upset by having awakened in Brandon's bed. She was still fully dressed and nothing had happened. Yet, the very idea of being in his bed disturbed her. After all, they had important business to conduct and the thought that he had let her sleep precious time away once again was upsetting. Every spare second had to be spent in the effort to get Sweet back to her.

As Sash moved down the hallway the house seemed eerily quiet. She wondered if there were others in the house beside Brandon and her. Closed doors lined the hallway on both sides. Adorning the walls between the doors were oil and acrylic paintings, all originals. It crossed her mind that Brandon might be behind one of the closed doors that she was passing. Turning the doorknob on the last door at the top of the stairway, she was about to open it to see if he was inside when a strident voice stopped her.

"Good, you're up."

Startled, Sash turned to find Brandon standing in the doorway of one of the rooms that she had just passed. There was a sense of urgency in his voice, but Sash hardly noticed. She was much too preoccupied with the transition in his appearance. He stood before her resplendent in a finely tailored tuxedo that fit him impeccably. The crisp white shirt that he wore was pleated and outlined his broad chest. The black bow tie he wore was plain, but the cologne he wore was not. It was enticing, as enticing as he looked. Sash felt her stomach flutter. Silently she chided herself for the transgression.

"You scared me!" Flustered by her reaction to him, Sash took the defensive. "I was looking for you."

"Well here I am. I was about to wake you up. We've got to get going." Tossing his tuxedo jacket over his shoulder, Brandon closed the door behind him and walked over to Sash.

His cologne tantalized her senses. She clutched the brass doorknob she had been about to turn in an attempt to steady herself. "Where are we going?"

"Out." Without further explanation, Brandon grabbed Sash by the elbow and started shuttling her down the stairs at a mini gallop.

Protesting, Sash pulled away. "Out where? This *is* your house isn't it?"

Looking up at her with an impatient glare, Brandon nodded.

"Then why are you dressed like that? Why did you bring me here? Tell me something or I'm not taking another step! *And* if you haven't noticed I don't have any shoes on!" Her mouth formed a defiant pout.

Brandon didn't have time to argue. "We're going out to get more money." Turning, he continued down the stairs confident that Sash would follow. He was right.

They stepped into a cavernous ultra modern living room flooded with recessed lighting beaming from the cathedral ceiling. Decorated in contemporary furnishings, there were enough windows to allow gazing into the distance at the lights of the city beyond and enough skylights to allow gazing upward at the multitude of stars above. The effect was dramatic and romantic, neither of which Sash would of thought of if she were to describe Brandon Plaine. She watched as he went to the set of windows and peeked out.

Still disconcerted by his handsome appearance Sash asked, "Again, why are we here? Why are you dressed like that? And what do you mean by out to get *more* money?"

Brandon looked at her over his shoulder. "We're going to a dinner dance. I'm expecting our ride to pull up any minute. Go get your shoes on." He turned back to the window. Sash ignored his command.

"To a dinner dance?" Her eyes swept her wrinkled attire, then returned to his impeccable appearance. "You must be crazy! We don't have time to go to any dinner dance. You may have forgotten but there's a little boy out there in danger and the only place I'm going is out to find him. And furthermore, I want to know why we are here at your place?"

Brandon looked at Sash's thunderous expression and gave a frustrated sigh. This was the most obstinate woman on earth. One would think that it was *him* asking *her* for a million dollars worth of help, not vice versa. No, two million dollars worth!

He filled her in on the telephone call from the kidnappers and the additional monetary demand. He watched her expression carefully as he paused to let his words sink in. She appeared to be as stunned by this latest development as he had been. He continued. "As for why we're going to this party it's like I said. I might be able to get the rest of the money for your brother's release at the party since I can't reach my contacts. Now, if you're through playing twenty questions go get your shoes on. Our ride is here."

* * *

The ride turned out to be a limousine that was to take them to the dance, but first there was a detour to the House of Isis. On the way Brandon explained the reason for both detours.

"There's this guy I know, Sinclair Reasoner. He and his wife are giving this bash tonight to honor the people who volunteer for the foundation he founded. I got the invitation weeks ago, but I hadn't planned on going. Now I feel that he might be able to lend me the money. So I want to talk to him face to face."

Sash fought her rising panic. "You're not going to tell him why you need the money are you?"

"I'll be as vague as possible..."

"I don't care how vague you're going to be. There's no way of asking someone for that kind of money without them asking why."

"Whatever I borrow from him, he knows I'm good for it. I won't have to go into a lot of explanations."

"Let me get this straight. You're going to borrow close to a million dollars from this man and you're not going to tell him why, and he won't ask?" Sash didn't hide her skepticism. "Anyway, what makes you think he's got that kind of money lying around? You don't."

Brandon bristled at Sash's dig. He wasn't used to being questioned. "Do you have a better plan? If so, let me know. Remember it was you who told me to *channel my energy* in a new direction." He turned to look at the passing scenery.

Sash recognized her own words being flung back at her and she knew that her criticism upset Brandon. That had not been her intention. She had known this man for less than 24 hours and had been forced to put more trust in him than she had put in any man. He was making every effort to help her despite his doubts. Yet, over the past few hours she hadn't done much to show her gratitude.

Sash touched his arm, and waited until Brandon turned to her before speaking. "I'm sorry. I didn't mean to sound so ungrateful. But a thought just occurred to me that might help. Some banks have branches in grocery stores that are open on Sunday…"

"My bank doesn't."

"Oh," Sash's shoulders slumped even as her mind raced. "Maybe we can stall them until Monday, when you can get to your funds."

"I doubt it. Besides, I would think that you would want your brother back as soon as possible."

He was right. She didn't want Sweet to be endangered one more day than necessary.

"All right. We'll do it your way. Now tell me about this House of Isis."

Appeased, Brandon's mood brightened. "It's one of those places where women can get the full works, including buying clothes in the boutique. So I'll outfit you from head to toe."

"And I'll repay you."

Brandon started to protest, but stopped himself. "I called the owner and she's opening the shop for me. I told her we don't have much time, so she said that she can throw you together in about an hour."

"Throw me together?" Sash was amused at the description.. "All right, we'll see how well she can *throw me together*."

* * *

An hour and a half later as Brandon and Sash stood in

the entrance of the posh hotel ballroom where the dinner dance was being held, Sash assumed that she had been thrown together well judging from the looks that Brandon was giving her. She was pleased with the results. Her dreadlocks had been swept upward into a sleek, sophisticated hairstyle that did wonders for her appearance. The floor length gown she wore was simply cut and fitted her as if it were made for her. The tiny diamond earrings in her pierced ears along with the matching necklace both sparkled brightly against the contrast of her brown skin. Her makeup had been applied with such expertise that Sash looked and felt beautiful. Brandon's eyes had nearly popped out of his head when he first saw her and even now he couldn't seem to keep his eyes off of her. She felt pretty and it felt good. After the horror of these past few days she had never expected to feel good again until Sweet was back in her arms. Yet, she also felt guilty for feeling anything but sadness about the circumstances that brought them to this social event, and Sash fought the temptation of enjoying the moment.

As Brandon and Sash entered the ballroom in search of Sinclair Reasoner, he felt like an adolescent fool at the way he was ogling Sash. She had cleaned up well, *very* well and when she stepped into the lobby of the House of Isis where he had been waiting she had nearly taken his breath away. The gown that she wore was simple—white satin floor-length, with a fitted cut that accentuated her small waist and curvaceous hips. The bodice was cut off of one shoulder revealing a smooth expanse of brown skin. A woman whom Brandon had viewed as a moody, argumentative eccentric had been transformed into a gorgeous enchantress with the poise and grace of an African queen. It caught Brandon completely off guard.

It seemed as though Sash Adams was a chameleon, and if he could ever untie his tongue and regain control of his rising libido he could appreciate the fact. Right now he had to keep reminding himself of the reason why they were at this gathering.

Tearing his eyes from Sash, Brandon scanned the ballroom as he searched the crowd of bejeweled ladies and tuxedoed men. This gathering was far from the little bash that Brandon had expected it to be. Linen draped tables were scattered throughout the large room. Each table was adorned with fresh flower centerpieces and lighted candelabras. The band was live and scores of people were on the dance floor enjoying themselves. It was crowded.

"Do you see Mr. Reasoner?"

Sash's question brought Brandon's attention back to her. "No, I don't see him." Surveying the room once again, his eyes fell on a line of people at the buffet table. The rumble of his stomach reminded him of how long it had been since either of them had eaten. "Are you hungry?"

Sash was famished. Food had been all but forgotten during the course of her ordeal. "Yes, I am, but I don't think that we have time to…"

"Yes, we do." Brandon interrupted. He guided her further into the room toward the buffet line. "Neither one of us will be any good to your brother if we starve to death."

On the way to the buffet table Brandon was warmly greeted numerous times by party guest. Everyone seemed to know him.

"You certainly seem popular," Sash noted as they slipped into the back of the serving line.

"Not popular, just rich." Brandon's tone was flat.

Surprised by his statement Sash attempted to read his

expression, but his face was blank. "So money *can't* buy friends, huh?"

Brandon raised a brow. "You'd be surprise what money *can't* buy."

No, she wouldn't be surprised. She had witnessed first hand the power of money when she was with Michael. What she had witnessed she hadn't always liked; but for now money was the only way out of her dilemma.

"Brandon!"

The sound of his name brought the attention of both Brandon and Sash to the caramel colored beauty making her way through the crowd. As she floated toward the two of them dressed in a sea of blue chiffon, her light brown, shoulder length tresses danced on bare shoulders covered by delicate netting. Eyes nearly the same shade as her creamy complexion sparkled unabashedly at the sight of the man on whom all of her attention was focused. Reaching Brandon, she caressed his face fondly with manicured fingers and placed a familiar kiss on his lips.

"I didn't know that you would be here. I heard through the grapevine that you weren't coming." Her welcoming smile told of her pleasure at his having reversed his decision.

"Valerie." Brandon's greeting was less than enthusiastic, but it didn't seem to faze her. The expression on her face never changed.

"How have you been?" Valerie's inquiry appeared to be sincere.

Brandon knew better and wanted to rail at her and ask her what did she care? They had parted months ago under less then amicable circumstances. There wasn't a person in this room who was more of an example of what money could buy. Three divorces from very wealthy husbands could attest to that. She had targeted Brandon as husband number four, but he had not minced words when he informed her that marriage between them wasn't going to happen. Her response had been less than lady like.

The unexpected kiss that she had bestowed on him in greeting was both unwelcome and unwanted. He had enough on his hands at the moment. Right now his fondest wish was that Valerie Simmons simply vanish back into the crowd.

As Brandon and the woman stood gawking at each other, Sash could feel the tension between them. The cause wasn't difficult to discern. The woman wanted Brandon, but he didn't want her. Apparently this woman didn't get the message. It would have been fun standing there and watching the interaction between them, but unfortunately Sash couldn't afford the indulgence. She had more important things on her mind. She cleared her throat drawing attention from both parties. Brandon did the introductions

"Valerie, this is Sash Adams. Sash, Valerie Simmons."

Flashing a friendly smile, Sash extended her hand. "Nice meeting you, Valerie. I like your dress."

Valerie looked from Sash to Brandon quickly assessing the situation between the two of them before switching her attention back to Sash. She raised a disapproving brow at the locked tresses piled atop Sash's head then limply shook her outstretched hand.

"Hello." Her greeting for Sash was about as enthusiastic as the one Valerie had received from Brandon. If she had deemed it important Sash would have subtly reassured Valerie that she was no threat to her regarding Brandon, but time was short. Perhaps Valerie could serve a better purpose.

"Valerie, maybe you can help us. I'm anxious to meet the man who is hosting this lovely affair. Do you know Mr. Reasoner?"

"Of course I do." Valerie looked at Sash as if she couldn't believe she could ask such a stupid question. "I know Sinclair and his wife, Nedra. Brandon hasn't introduced you?" She looked at Brandon questioningly. He answered her look with a nonchalant shrug.

"Well have you seen him around here anyplace?" Sash refocused Valerie's attention, anxious to get to Reasoner. "If so, perhaps you can point him out."

"I just spoke to Sinclair and Nedra. I passed them going out on the patio a few minutes ago." Valerie delivered the information with an air of superiority that changed to one of surprise as Sash and Brandon offered their thanks then abruptly took off across the room.

CHAPTER 7

Sash sat at the table opposite Nedra Reasoner and tried to be attentive. This beautiful woman with the striking beige eyes had been nothing less than kind since Brandon had introduced Sash to her and her husband, Sinclair. That had been thirty minutes ago. She and Brandon had tracked the couple down and found them in an isolated section of the garden engaged in a passionate embrace. Presently, Brandon and Sinclair were still there talking. Nedra had invited Sash to join her at her table after Brandon unceremoniously dismissed Sash from the garden. Wanting to be a part of the conversation, she had been stung by his dismissal. She had wanted to assure herself that Brandon would reveal nothing that might endanger Sweet's life. Nevertheless, his overbearing attitude was an issue between them and it was one she was determined to address.

"You haven't eaten much," Nedra noted as she glanced at Sash's plate. "Brandon said that you were half starved."

She gave her hostess a small smile. "Well actually he's right. I am hungry." Sash took her fork, speared a broccoli flower and popped it in her mouth.

Nedra returned her smile. "I hope that you weren't embarrassed by what happened in the garden."

Sash furrowed her brows in silent question, wondering if Nedra, too, had been disturbed by Brandon's abrupt dismissal of her from the garden. Nedra saw the question in her expression.

"I'm talking about my husband and me getting caught making out," she explained. "I guess we should be the ones embarrassed."

Sash grinned. "I'm guessing that you're not." She and Brandon had offered profound apologies at their interruption of the intimate moment, but the couple hadn't seemed too disturbed.

Nedra shrugged. "Nope! The man is fine as he wants to be and I love him to death. Girl, I can't keep my hands off of him."

The two women shared a hearty laugh. It felt good to Sash. For a moment her mind was not preoccupied with what was happening in the garden.

* * *

"Man, I can help you out with about $100,000 immediately," Sinclair said to Brandon. "But let me make a few phone calls and I should be able to raise a bit more. How much do you need to close this business deal?"

"Close to a million."

"A million, huh? Well, I never thought I'd need that much money this weekend." Sinclair Reasoner's handsome face lit up in amusement at his attempt at humor.

"Neither did I," Brandon concurred dryly. "But this deal came up unexpectedly and like I said, I can't get access to my accounts until Monday. I don't want the deal to fall through. It's very important."

Sinclair shook his head in empathy, then quietly studied Brandon. The two men sat across from each other on stone benches in a secluded section of the fragrant flower garden. A haunting melody drifted from the hotel ballroom. Sinclair's attention shifted to the music for a moment before he transferred it back to Brandon.

"What's really up, man?" he asked looking Brandon in the eye. "I sense that there's more behind your needing this money than what you're telling me. Are you in some kind of trouble?"

Brandon was impressed by his intuitiveness. He liked and respected this man. In addition, he trusted him. Much of his adult life, Brandon had isolated himself from personal involvement. He had experienced too much betrayal in his life to become overly involved with others, and he didn't trust too many people. Given the present situation that he found himself in with Sash he needed to talk to someone. If she was involved in trying to swindle money from him maybe an objective party could sort out her story and see things more clearly than he. Maybe if he shared this situation with ....

Brandon took a deep breath. "Sin," he started, addressing his friend by his nickname, "You and Nedra have three kids and you love them. Right?"

"We would die for them."

"Suppose you had to depend on a perfect stranger to save the life of one of your kids?"

Sinclair frowned. "What do you mean? Like with an organ transplant or something?"

"No, nothing like that." Brandon paused, uncertain as to

how he should proceed. Would what he was about to reveal sound as incredulous to Sinclair as it did to him? Yet, he was living the incredible and the burden of this child's life possibly being in his hands spurred him on. "You see, earlier today…"

"Brandon."

Brandon started at the sound of Sash's voice. He looked up to see her standing on the paved pathway leading into the garden area where he and Sinclair sat talking.

"I'm sorry. Did I disturb you?" Her voice was steady as she glared at Brandon suspiciously.

"No, we were just winding up." Brandon returned her malevolent scowl. She wasn't going to make him feel guilty.

Brandon and Sinclair rose as Sash drew closer. Her eyes darted from one man to another. "Is everything all right?" There was subtext in her question that Brandon caught immediately.

"Everything is just fine," he reassured her.

Brandon came to her and placed a hand on the small of her back, momentarily distracting her. She inhaled and regained her focus. She had the disquieting feeling when she approached the two men that she had interrupted an important moment. She hoped it wasn't what she feared.

While sitting in the ballroom Sash had become increasingly apprehensive about the meeting that was taking place in the garden. The fact that Brandon had to go to someone else for the needed funds already increased the chance of revelation. She simply didn't trust Brandon not to tell his friend about the abduction and ransom demand. With that in mind she had made her appearance in the garden. She didn't care whether Brandon liked it or not. Sometimes she couldn't believe her bad luck. Who on earth but her would have to depend on a multimillionaire who couldn't get his hands on an extra million dollars?

Brandon started to escort Sash from the garden. Sinclair called after them, "Stop by my place at 8:00 tomorrow morning and I'll have that information for you." Brandon thanked him.

As they entered the ballroom, Sash could tell that Brandon was disturbed by her sudden appearance in the garden. But if she interrupted his little tryst with Sinclair before he spilled the beans she was glad that she did it.

They worked their way through the ballroom toward the entrance as the band started playing a popular love song that brought those seated at the tables up on their feet. Sash and Brandon found themselves swept up in the momentum and ended up on the dance floor. With an accepting shrug, Brandon turned and gathered Sash in his arms. She resisted.

"What are you doing? We've got to go."

"And do what?" Brandon tightened his hold, drawing her close. "Nothing else can be done until tomorrow anyway. Just relax."

Sash looked at Brandon and rolled her eyes. That was easier said than done. She was in the bowels of hell barely holding on to her sanity and he wanted to stop for a dance. She wanted to talk to him about what he said to Reasoner. It was clear that his friend was going to loan him the money, but she had to know exactly what Brandon had told him about his need for the money.

"Look, we need to talk." Sash's voice rose above the din of the music. She felt desperate as they danced smoothly in time to the music. The heat from his body invaded her pores. She could feel the ripple of his muscles beneath her fingers as they flexed nervously on his back. Brandon was too close and it was unsettling. As if reading her mind, Brandon pulled Sash closer. She felt weak, needy, wanting. As close as they were she could feel his want too. It was *quite* evident. Startled, Sash pulled away.

"Obviously my brother's situation doesn't bother you, Brandon, but it does bother me and I'm afraid that I can't enjoy dancing as long as Sweet is God knows where. Go on and have your fun, but you'll do it by yourself."

Prying herself out of Brandon's arms, Sash pushed her way through the crowd toward the entranceway. The room had turned stifling, and she needed a breath of fresh air. As she reached the front door and made her way outside she wondered how she had managed to stay sane and standing these last couple of days. Nothing was going the way she thought it would, and now Brandon was teasing her, titillating her senses. This was something that she just didn't need.

Sash stood outside the hotel trying to figure out what to do next. She and Brandon had come to the affair in a limousine, which meant that she would have to take a cab home. But then what?

"You forgot this."

Sash felt the weight of the satin cape that matched her dress as it was draped across her shoulders. She turned to meet Brandon's waiting eyes. He didn't look pleased. Well, neither was she.

"Get away from me, Brandon. I don't have time for your game playing." Sash turned away from him. He had practically seduced her on the dance floor and her body was still tingling from the effect.

Brandon signaled for the limousine. When it pulled up

and the chauffeur opened the door for them he slid in and held out his hand for Sash to join him. She folded her arms across her chest and stood there ignoring his gesture. Brandon decided to use a bit of bribery. "Do you want to know exactly what I said to Sinclair or not?"

He hit the mark immediately. Heaving a reluctant sigh, Sash pushed aside his outstretched hand as she slid in beside him. Brandon managed to hide his triumphant smile as the limo door closed behind her.

As they rode along, Sash was determined that she was not going to beg Brandon for the information she needed. Being at his mercy for her brother's life was demeaning enough. If there was any other way to get Sweet back other than going to the authorities she would take it. If only she had enough time to contact Michael. Brandon's voice broke her concentration.

"I know you want to know if I told Sinclair about Sweet, and the answer is no, but I was tempted to tell him. I used the excuse that I needed the money because of an opportunity to get in on a business deal. He said that he had $100,000 cash that he can loan me. As you heard, he'll have it for me tomorrow morning."

"But that still makes you short on cash."

"That's true, but don't worry. I've got an idea."

"Another one?"

Brandon overlooked her sarcasm. "I've tried everything I could think of to appease these criminals, but I think its time to face the fact that the authorities have to be contacted."

Her answer was definitive. "No. That's not an option."

Brandon looked at Sash intently. "Then you need to ask yourself some hard questions. Like what are you going to do if I do get all of the money, make the drop and they don't give your brother back to you?"

Sash gave Brandon a look that could kill. "That's not going to happen." *It couldn't.*

"Be realistic, there's nothing to stop it from happening. I know that you won't like this but it seems to me as if you're compromising your brother's life by not involving the authorities."

"I'm not compromising Sweet's life. I'm trying to save it." With a clenched jaw, Sash turned to look out the window.

Brandon could see that she had shut him out. It was time to take off the gloves. Brandon turned his entire body to face Sash. "You accused me of playing games earlier, but let me reassure you, I don't. What we're doing is deadly serious." He paused for a second to assess what he was about to say, then continued. "Suppose I told you that I have already called the authorities? Suppose everything I've done since we left your apartment has being monitored by them?"

Sash forced herself not to react to Brandon's words. Could she have been wrong about him? She studied the sharp planes of his face. His expression was unreadable, leaving her to wonder if he was telling the truth. Had he really called the authorities?

In the short time that Sash had known him she had to depend on her instincts to discern whether she could trust Brandon. She depended on those instincts not to fail her. If they did, then she would be failing Sweet.

"Please tell the driver to pull over so that I can get out of this limo."

"What?" Brandon croaked, shocked at her request. "Why do you want to get out?"

"If you're in cahoots with the cops then let me out right now. You've just said that I can't trust you. So I won't trust you and I refuse to go any further with you. I'll do what I have to do on my own to get Sweet back, no matter what it takes. So stop this limo and let me out right now."

Brandon looked out the window at the passing landscape. It was desolate. "You can't get out here! We're miles from my house and your apartment."

"Let me out, Brandon, unless you want to be charged with kidnapping. And wouldn't *that* be ironic."

"But it's dark! Anything could happen to you."

"What do you care?" Sash reached for the car door handle. With catlike reflexes Brandon moved to stop her, pinning her against the cushioned softness of the limo's leather seat.

"Don't do that, Sash! I can't let you out of here!"

Angered by his bullying tactics, Sash struggled to free herself. Her effort was unsuccessful, increasing her frustration.

"I told you no. So stop that!" Brandon demanded, knowing that she had no defense against his superior strength. But she did have fingernails—not as long and strong as they had been, but just as lethal. Without hesitation she used them. With a pain filled yelp, Brandon released her.

"What did you do that for?" He sounded like a hurt child as he nursed the wounds on his hand. "That hurt!"

"It was meant to hurt. I refuse to stay in this car with a man who would help kill my brother. I'm getting out of this limo and there's nothing you can do to stop me."

Taking advantage of the limo having stopped at a red light, Sash reached for the door handle. Once again, Brandon made a move to stop her, but his time his tactic was different. Grabbing her by the shoulders, he turned her around, pulled her to him and stopped her actions with a kiss.

Sash stiffened, shocked and surprised by the sudden contact. Clamping her lips together tightly, she refused him entrance; but Brandon was persistent. His insistent tongue toyed with her determined lips. Slowly, steadily her eyes drifted close and her lips allowed him entrance. Once inside Brandon took control. His tongue teased and taunted Sash with a kiss so thoroughly erotic that it left her weak. Then as suddenly as it had begun, the kiss was over. Brandon pulled away.

Dazed, Sash's eyes fluttered open. She looked up at Brandon, stunned. He sat back in his seat looking much too pleased with himself, waiting for her reaction. She wiped the kiss from her lips with the back of her hand as her anger flared anew. "You had no right to do that!"

"Yes, you're right, I didn't. But you liked it."

Brandon's reply was delivered with so much arrogance that Sash wanted to slap him. Instead, she fought fire with fire. "So did you."

Brandon blinked, caught off guard by her perspective comeback. "You think so, do you?"

Sash looked at him with a confidence so absolute that it left Brandon feeling unsteady, much as their kiss had. Sash was much too sure of herself. He was a man whose wealth and power had made grown men tremble. In some situations he could snap his fingers and have people jump to his command, but Sash didn't seem to be intimidated by him in any way. All day she had challenged him, defied him, affected and, yes, attracted him in ways that left him feeling uneasy. He had known Sash Adams less than twenty-four hours and during this time she had left his body hot and bothered, his mind muddled and confused. She threatened to invade forbidden places inside his heart and he couldn't allow that. So he lied.

"Nope, I didn't like it." His tone was frosty. "I just took advantage of an opportunity. Sort of like what you're doing with me."

Overlooking his veiled insult, once again Sash called his bluff. "You're lying and you know it." To emphasize her point she glanced down briefly at the telltale bulge in his pants, then back up at him. She smiled knowingly.

Brandon turned away from her, and stared out of the window not wanting her to see the truth in his eyes. This woman was conceited…incorrigible… He had been a happy man this morning—young successful, rich and in control of his world. He hadn't asked for Sash Adams to enter his life and make him feel guilty about her brother, make him feel… What? Her voice snapped him out of his reverie.

"I'm still getting out of this limo if you called the police. So don't think that some little smooch is going to change that." Sash frowned. "So, did you call them or not?"

"No," Brandon answered half listening as his eyes stayed riveted to the driver's exterior rearview mirror. Suddenly, he leaned forward and pressed the intercom.

"Driver, hit the next exit and don't signal when you exit." Brandon leaned back in his seat. He was tense. Sash sat straight up.

"What's going on?" She looked out the back window to see what had caught his attention.

"I think we're being followed."

In the distance she could see the headlights behind them. Sash closed her eyes and prepared herself for what was to come next. It looked as though there would be no peace for either of them tonight.

The driver took the exit as instructed, then a sharp right turn that had the tires squealing and set Sash's heart beating like a tom-tom. Brandon continued to rattle off directions while she kept watch out the back window. The headlights disappeared for a few seconds, then reappeared without warning.

"I'm not sure but I think that they're still behind us," Sash's voice was strong, determined, unwavering.

Brandon took a quick look over his shoulder to observe two tiny points of light in motion. "It could be, but..." He returned his attention to what lay ahead. They were coming to a four-way intersection where a yellow light was turning red. There were no other cars on the street. "Driver, keep going until you get to the Monterey airport. Park anywhere there for fifteen minutes, then drive back to the garage."

When the limo stopped, without warning Sash found herself being jerked from the limo and running unceremoniously through the city streets. The sound of their heavy breathing and the click clack of her high heels beating against the sidewalk echoed loudly in the quiet night. Along the way, she shed the heels, giving her a better running advantage. Gripping the shoes in one hand and Brandon's large hand with the other, she kept pace as he pulled her through the well-lit streets until they took a detour into a dark alleyway.

"Where are we going?" Her breath came in painful gasps as Sash silently berated herself for having abandoned her workout routine.

"Through here." Brandon was noncommittal as he tried to find his bearings. He really wasn't sure where they were or where they were going, but an instinct for survival was compelling him to go forward.

"Stop!" Sash yelled louder than she had intended, but

her words had their intended effect. Brandon came to an abrupt halt. She jerked her hand free of his.

"What in the hell are we doing? Why are we running through this alley like idiots? Wouldn't it have been safer to stay in the limo?"

Brandon was miffed. "I don't know, Sash. You tell me? How did they know that we were in the limo? I used it as transportation deliberately so that we wouldn't be followed from my house. Yet, somehow they knew where we were and what limo to follow. Now, I wasn't with you the entire time we were at the dance. So I trusted you. Was I wrong?"

Sash's eyes widened. The accusation couldn't get more deliberate. "Surely, you don't think..."

Brandon's eyes narrowed. "What, Sash? That you might have called your friends?"

"How dare you! You...you..."

The satin slipper barely missed Brandon's head. He ducked just in time. Furious, he caught her by the wrist as she prepared to take another swing. He pulled her firmly toward him. They stood chest to chest.

"I warn you, lady, don't ever try to hit me again." His tone was ominous, but Sash didn't blink.

"And don't you *ever* accuse me of something so vile again!" She jerked away from him and took a step back. "I'm telling you for the very last time. I had *nothing* to do with my brother's kidnapping. I don't know these people or why they're following us, but if you still don't trust or believe me there's nothing else I can do about it."

With that she turned and walked back toward the lighted street. Despite his anger, Brandon couldn't help but be amused by the picture that she made—barefoot, her dress hiked up and her dreads in disarray. Yet, still she walked with the dignity of a queen. Sash Adams was quite a woman. Maybe he had been wrong about suspecting her of complicity. He had to confess to having become increasingly paranoid over the past few hours. Who knows, maybe the car behind them hadn't been following them at all.

Suddenly, a thought hit him like a ton of bricks. The person following them could have been a member of his own staff. He'd been on John to step up security. If it was one of his men, Brandon had made a big mistake accusing Sash.

Taking a deep breath, he prepared himself for the verbal fire he knew could come if he tried to make amends with her. "Hold up. I'm not sure where we are."

"We're in Carmel not far from the shopping center on Ocean Avenue." She answered confidently never missing a step.

Sheepishly, Brandon followed her, unsure as to who was in charge at this point. They were about to step out of the alley onto the street when a slow moving car drew their attention. Simultaneously, they both stepped back into the shadows. With their backs pressed against the bricks of the building they tried hard to become invisible. Both pair of eyes followed the vehicle's progress until it vanished into the night. With a sigh of relief, Sash stepped out onto the sidewalk.

"I doubt if anybody would be following us in that," said Brandon, his tone offering a plea for reconciliation. The car had been a Rolls Royce. Sash ignored him and kept walking. Brandon traipsed along behind her.

The flicker of a yellow warning light illuminated the two well-dressed figures as they walked along the silent street. Their cautious strides were a testimony to the unspoken fears that each one harbored.

CHAPTER 8

Sash sank deep into the cushioned softness of the accent chair that sat opposite the matching sofa Brandon occupied. They had taken refuge in the luxurious suite of a quaint hotel back in Monterey close to his business office. Tired of playing hide and seek through the streets of Carmel, Brandon had called a taxi on his cell phone and had directed it to their present destination. On the way he had explained to Sash that the suite had only recently been acquired. It was to be used as a haven when he was too tired to drive home from work. "As far as I know, nobody knows about it," he assured her.

Sash silently questioned that statement when he produced a pair of women's jeans and a tailored blouse for her to change into. In the taxi he had apologized profusely for his earlier accusation. He blamed it on the paranoia he had acquired as a result of the events of the day. She started not to forgive him, but again felt caught between a rock and a hard place. There was no one else on whom she could depend to help her free her brother. So she accepted his apology, although the words he had uttered in the alley put her on alert. He continued not to trust her and she was no longer certain that she could trust him.

When Sash came out of the room after changing from her gown, Brandon was on his cell phone winding up a conversation. She made an inquiry regarding the call and he said that he was checking his telephone messages. She accepted his explanation but remained on guard. As for now, she was enjoying her present surroundings and was glad for the temporary respite. The tensions of the evening had lessened somewhat and she felt much more relaxed.

She looked over at Brandon. He had changed into a pair of jeans and a shirt and he lay sprawled on the sofa with his eyes closed. One arm was flung across his forehead. Although she felt refreshed, he looked exhausted. It had been quite a day for them both.

"Why do you think we were being followed?"

"I don't know." Brandon didn't open his eyes.

Sash looked at him thoughtfully. "Obviously the kidnappers are stupid. You would think that anyone who snatches a child would keep a low profile, not go around following people."

"You would think."

"There must be something else going on, but I can't imagine what."

"Uh huh." Brandon remained noncommittal. He didn't want to talk about it because he knew who had been following them. When they arrived at the hotel he had called John who confirmed that it was, indeed, his security men who had gotten a little too close. It was best if that incident was forgotten, but she wouldn't it go.

"I hurt one of the kidnappers badly, so there should be

only one of them left following us." Sash got up from her seat and began to wander. "But I'm not certain."

Alerted by her movements, Brandon opened his eyes and through heavy lids watched as she padded barefoot around the room examining knick-knacks. He sensed that her restlessness masked her apprehension, but he was glad that she was preoccupied with something else. However, there were some things that did need to be discussed further and this was a good time for it.

"You know, Sash, I've been thinking. I hope you don't mind if I ask you something."

Tensing, she stopped her exploration and turned. "What?"

"You're thirty-four, right?"

"I'm thirty-five." She relaxed.

"And your brother is five?"

"Is that the question?" Sash chuckled. She knew where this was leading.

"Well no," Brandon hesitated. "I was just wondering how old your parents were when they had your brother?"

"I thought that would come up. I'm used to being asked that question and I always give the same answer. They were old enough to know better."

It was Brandon's turn to chuckle. The lady had a sense of humor. "Do the two of you have other brothers and sisters?"

"My stepfather had a daughter, but she died."

"I see," Brandon digested the information. He noticed that there had been a slight shift in her body language and a slight hesitation before she answered his question. "Were you and his daughter close?"

Sash shook her head. "No, I only met her once."

Brandon nodded, curious as to why she and her stepsister only met once, but he'd find out more about that later. "Tell me about your little brother. What kind of kid is he?"

Sash smiled as she thought about Sweet. She described for Brandon the little boy with the impish grin who could charm his way out of almost anything. "He's so full of energy it's hard to keep up with him. He's all boy, that's for sure. Ice cream is his favorite food and he loves all kinds of sports. I'm going to sign him up for t-ball when I find a job and get settled." She told Brandon how well he did in preschool and what a whiz he was in kindergarten. "Sweet likes doing yoga with me and he likes it when I plant kisses all over his face, even though he wipes them away with both hands—that's our little ritual. He loves animals and nature and he swims like a fish."

Sash stopped abruptly as she felt her chest constrict. She took a deep breath and pulled herself together. "He's a wonderful little boy and I love him very much." The last words were delivered in a choked whisper.

"He sounds like a great kid."

"Yes, he is." Sash agreed, closing the subject to keep from falling apart. She wandered over to where Brandon was sitting, patted his feet aside and sat down next to him on the sofa. He curled his long legs up as comfortably as he could to make room for her.

"Brandon, we have to come up with a plan for tomorrow."

"No need. I've got one. In the morning I'll call Sinclair, go get the money he's loaning me and I'll have the rest of the money I left at my house delivered to my office. Then we'll go there and wait for the call telling me where to drop the ransom."

Sash yawned, kicked off her shoes and curled on the sofa, her legs pressed against his. "Well it's a plan, but let me remind you that you still won't have all of the money."

"Don't worry about it. I've got a plan for that too." Stretching out, he snuggled down deeper into the sofa.

"Let me hear it." Sash got comfortable as well.

Brandon mumbled something unintelligible, his eyes fluttered close and instantly he was asleep. Sash sighed. It looked as though she would have to find out about the latest plan tomorrow.

Finding extra bedding in a nearby linen closet, she covered Brandon and turned the lamp out on the table next to the sofa. Starting toward her bedroom, Sash hesitated, turned and went back to where Brandon lay sleeping. Leaning over him, she planted a kiss on his cheek. The man was arrogant, stubborn and too domineering for her taste. Only a short while ago she wanted to brain him. Yet, he was willing to help her, even though he still harbored doubts, and she was grateful for that.

Today had been difficult, but they were at peace with each other tonight. The way things had been going so far who knew what tomorrow would bring.

* * *

The morning found Sash sitting in Brandon's office with him waiting for the telephone call that would give Sweet his freedom. She sat in the same leather wingback chair in which she had sat yesterday, watching the clock nervously, willing the telephone to ring. It was 8:15 in the morning. The call was to come at 9:00 a.m..

"Watching the clock won't make the time go faster." Brandon sat in his chair at the rolltop desk watching Sash. Although his words to her didn't indicate it, his thoughts were not on the time of day. He was remembering the feel of a warm pair of lips against his cheek. Had he been dreaming or had Sash really kissed him last night? He was a light sleeper and had been awakened as she placed a blanket over him. He had been lulled back into slumber when a moment later he could feel the heat of her body close to his. The kiss was quick, and not on his lips, but if it was a dream it was a pleasant one. If it wasn't he enjoyed the unexpected turn of events even more. He didn't know what would have possessed her, but why should he complain?

Earlier this morning at the hotel they had enjoyed a pleasant camaraderie, until he made the call to Sinclair. Brandon made arrangements to pick up the money he had borrowed, then told Sash his plan for the ransom money. The good feelings between them quickly eroded and she wasn't shy about expressing her disagreement with his decision. Even now as they sat in his office waiting for the call, Sash questioned his reasoning.

"I still don't see how this thing is going to work," Sash told him for the tenth time since he revealed to her what she felt was a dumb idea. "You can't be sure that they won't know that there's not two million dollars in those shopping bags!

"Like I've said, what I have planned will work."

"You don't know that! And who was that man who brought you the money from your house? Did he know what was in the briefcase? Does he know what's happening?"

"He's an employee. I'm his boss. He does what I ask him to do."

Sash shook her head. "There are too many people becoming involved. I don't..."

"I know. You don't like it. You keep telling me." Brandon gave a patient sigh. "Sinclair was able to come up with a quarter of a million dollars on short notice, and with the money I already have that should be enough to make it look like two million dollars. I find it hard to believe that these people we're dealing with have ever seen that much money in cash. I really don't think we're working with the smartest of criminals here. Anyway, I've got the cash, no matter how much it is, and they want it. My demand will be that they've got to have the boy with them. We have to see him and there has to be an even exchange, or there's no deal. That being the case, they won't have time to count the money."

Sash heard the confidence in his voice and tried to feel optimistic. Picking up one of the newspapers scattered on his desk she began to rifle through it. The newspaper shook visibly in her trembling hands.

"Things will work out like they're suppose to, Sash," he reassured her. "Take my word for it."

Sash still wasn't convinced. "Why should I? You don't know what's going to happen. If you're so smart tell me why there's no mention of the police finding the man at that house in Santa Cruz? He was hurt badly. I called 911 from a phone booth. Shouldn't somebody have found him by now and reported it? You would think it would be in one of these newspapers or on t.v.!"

"I told you, my people said that nothing has been on the wire."

"Then tell them to go check it out! You're good at giving orders." Sash tossed the newspaper aside. "I don't understand it. None of it." She got up from the chair and began pacing the room under Brandon's watchful eye. "And I don't like this waiting either. I can't sit still. I don't see how you can be so calm."

"I'm a newspaper man. Calm is my middle name."

Sash didn't react to Brandon's attempt at humor as she examined the numerous framed copies of *The Call* newspaper adorning the walls. Each edition was a framed front page chronicling some important African American event. Other than that, the walls were bare. There were no awards, no citations and she was sure that he must have earned plenty. Nothing in his office indicated anything personal about its occupant except the photograph on Brandon's desk—the one of him and the older man. Sash walked over and examined it.

"Is this your father?"

Brandon nodded. She noted a flash of sadness in his eyes before he lowered them.

Sash's eyes swept the handsome youth standing beside the man. Although the man appeared elated by the large fish they exhibited between them, the same pleasure wasn't reflected in the young man's eyes as they stared back at Sash.

"You look young in this picture. What were you fifteen? Sixteen? "

Brandon turned the brass frame holding the photo toward him, "Eighteen, but that's not me. I'm the one taking the picture."

Surprised by the revelation, Sash had opened her mouth to ask who was in the picture when a sound in the outer office caught their attention. Holding up his hand to warn Sash to be silent, Brandon rose and stole quietly to the door. Sash was close behind him. Opening the door a crack, he peered into the outer office to find the source of the sound. Brandon's body relaxed visibly as he opened the door fully. A smile replaced the tension on his face.

Sash peeked around his body to see its source. An attractive middle aged woman who appeared to be in her forties stood in the middle of the room. She looked startled.

"Mr. Plaine! You scared me."

"Hi, Mrs. Joseph. What are you doing here?"

"I'm trying to get that data base I was working on yesterday completed." The woman's eyes shifted to Sash.

"Mrs. Joseph, this is Sash Adams, Sash this is Mrs. Joseph." Brandon guided Sash in front of him as he spoke. "Mrs. Joseph is my executive assistant."

"Nice meeting you, Mrs. Joseph," Sash extended her hand in greeting.

"Ms. Adams." Her greeting was hesitant as she shook Sash's hand and scrutinized her closely. "Sash Adams. Sash Adams. Where have I hear your name before?" Realization dawned. "Sash Adams! You called here several times yesterday." Her attention switched back to Brandon. Her eyes were accusing this time, remembering his many rejections of Sash Adams' calls. She raised her brows in question. Brandon looked sheepish.

"Uh, well Mrs. Joseph, you don't have to bother with that data base today. You can do it on Monday." Brandon started moving her out of the office. Surprised at his action, the woman was resistant.

"But, if I wait until Monday, I'll be even more behind, I need to…."

"Don't worry about it, I'll hire a temp to help you catch up if necessary."

"But, Mr. Plaine, your regular assistant told me that I needed to..."

"I said don't worry about it. You're supposed to be off celebrating today. You don't need to be in here." He had hustled her to the front door by this time. He opened it.

"It's not the first holiday I've worked."

"All the more reason that you should be enjoying your weekend. You work too hard. Go enjoy your day." Brandon now stood in the front door blocking further entrance. His smile radiated empathy and concern, but Mrs. Joseph still seemed suspicious. Her eyes darted from Brandon to Sash, then back again.

"Well, all right, Mr. Plaine. If you say so." Mrs. Joseph turned to leave. "I'll see you on Monday." She looked back at Sash before leaving. "Nice meeting you, Ms. Adams." With one last questioning look at Brandon she was gone. He locked the door behind her.

"That was subtle." Sash leaned against the doorway leading into Brandon's office shaking her head at his actions. "She probably thinks that you and I are in here doing Lord knows what."

"Well, what did you want me to say? We're in here waiting for some kidnappers to call to tell us where to drop the ransom?" Brandon squeezed past her and went back into his office. "Mrs. J is cool. She's been with the company for some time."

Pushing away from the door, Sash followed him into his office. Brandon sat down at his desk. She returned to the wingback chair and glanced at the clock above his desk. It was 8:45.

"Fifteen minutes. Fifteen minutes before..." Sash let out

a shaky breath. "What are we doing, Brandon? How did we get here?"

Brandon chortled. "Lady, if you don't know I sure can't tell you. I certainly didn't ask to be here."

There was no arguing that. Sash sighed, trying to fight both fear and misery simultaneously. "These are dangerous people we're dealing with and we don't have all the money. Things could get shaky. I think some protection is needed, some kind of weapon."

"Don't worry about it. I've got it covered."

Sash's eyes flew to Brandon as fear took the forefront. "You're carrying a weapon? What? A gun? Where did you get it?"

"Don't worry about it."

"That's your favorite saying, isn't it?" Sash licked her parched lips. Her mouth was dry and she was beginning to feel nauseous. "That's okay for you to say, all you have to lose is money. *That* can be replaced."

Brandon could feel Sash's fear. It permeated the air. Yet, she still managed to maintain a strong facade. He still wasn't quite sure what to think about this woman, but the moment of truth was close for them both and there were realities that had to be faced.

"A life and death decision was made, Sash, the moment that you decided not to go to the authorities. While I understand your reason behind the decision you've made, it was foolish for me to go along with you and I pray that I didn't make a mistake. If I did, we'll know in a very short time."

Sash started to speak when Brandon's private telephone line rang. Both she and Brandon looked at the clock. It was 9:00 sharp. Brandon answered the call, pressing the speakerphone button. The voice was graveled, muffled. It was him.

"Listen to me carefully, I'm not going to repeat myself. Do you have the money?"

"Yes, I do have the money, but you won't get a thing unless you bring the boy with you and we have an even exchange."

"I'm making the rules around here, not you. " The voice was annoyed by the dictate. Sash looked at Brandon anxiously. He was unyielding.

"It's an even exchange or no exchange at all."

Sash held her breath. There was momentary silence, then, "No problem. Now listen carefully. There's a park in Monterey. The one with the kid's playground...."

* * *

Brandon parked his luxury SUV on the street outside of the park entrance at 12:45 p.m. He was to wait fifteen minutes, pick up the two shopping bags in which the money had been transferred, get out and follow the directions to the spot where he was to leave the ransom. According to the abductor Sweet would be at the drop site and visible as soon as Brandon delivered the money and walked away.

Brandon ran his hand through his hair. This entire thing was unnerving. He wanted to kick himself every time he thought about how he had allowed himself to get involved in this. Yesterday when he awakened the world was normal. Today it seemed beyond his control.

Brandon thought of Sash waiting back at his office. Would she be there when he returned? Brandon had been ordered to come alone when he made the drop. When the call was disconnected and Brandon informed Sash that he would comply with the demand she had hit the roof. They had spent the hours between the call and the drop arguing. She had demanded to be taken along, but he had left his office without her. He still wasn't sure that she wouldn't find some way to follow him. Sash had proven to be very resourceful. Something else that he liked about the lady. Actually, there were a lot of things he liked about Sash Adams. Too bad that they hadn't met under different circumstances.

Brandon checked his watch. It was time to go. Glancing over at the area near the park entrance he noticed parents sitting on benches absorbed in watching their children at play. Families were picnicking, bicycling, playing games and strolling, generally enjoying the holiday. People were everywhere and Brandon knew that out there somewhere, someone he didn't know—had never seen—was waiting and watching.

Slipping his sunglasses on, Brandon got out of the car and reached across the driver's seat to remove the bags. The car phone rang. Brandon froze. Glancing at caller I.D. he saw that the call was coming from his office. It had to be Sash. He had given her the number to appease her anger, fear and anxiety about what was occurring in the park. But why would she be calling him now? She knew the directions that were given to him and the time he was to proceed with the drop. Why would she pick such a bad time to call? Checking his watch again, he knew that he had to get started in order to be at his destination on time, but the telephone's constant ring held him there.

If he answered the call would the kidnappers be watching? Would they think something suspicious was happening? Should he take the chance? He started to remove the bags once again, hesitated, and then answered the telephone.

It was Sash and what she was saying was unintelligible. She sounded hysterical. Brandon's heart began to race.

"What the hell is it? What's wrong with you? Why are you calling me now?"

"Richmond! Richmond!"

"Richmond? What about Richmond? Are you insane? I've got to go!"

"A woman called from Richmond, California. She has Sweet with her. I talked to him. He's there. He's not in the park! We've got to get to Richmond! Now!"

After calming Sash with a promise to return to the office, Brandon disconnected the call and climbed back into his car with a heavy heart. The complexities of human beings never ceased to amaze him. Leaning his head back against the leather head rest, Brandon closed his eyes and saw Sash's lovely face. A little more than twenty-fours hours ago he didn't know that she existed, but in those few hours she had turned his world inside out. More than anything he wished that she hadn't made that last call. It would have been easier for him to walk into that park to face the unknown then to do what he had to do now.

Opening his eyes, Brandon gave a heavy sigh and pushed a number on his car phone. These last hours had been quite a ride, but now the ride was over.

CHAPTER 9

"Who are you working with, Ms. Adams?" The man's tone was meant to be intimidating but Sash continued to look through him as if he wasn't there. They were sitting in the conference room in Brandon's office and the man sat across the table from her. As he spoke he leaned close to her face in an effort to intimate her.

"You studied the law, Ms. Adams, so you're aware that extortion is a serious offense. I'm sure you wouldn't want to take the rap for this by yourself."

His breath smelled like sour spaghetti sauce, and Sash's empty stomach roiled, but she didn't move a muscle. She wasn't about to give him the satisfaction of acknowledging his existence. She hated him and she hated Brandon Plaine. It was he who was responsible for this stranger being here and interrogating her like some criminal. She was determined not to give either of them the satisfaction of letting them see that they affected her in any way. She felt alone, betrayed, abandoned. Right now misery was her only friend.

Sash had been sitting in Brandon's office awaiting his return from the park when she heard the front door open. Hurrying from the room certain that it was Brandon who had entered she was shocked when she was confronted by a burly black man who she recognized. He had acted as a courier earlier that morning delivering the money from Brandon's house to the office. The man was huge with the physique of a wrestler. He introduced himself as John Nathan explained to her that he was the head of Plaine Deal Media's security staff. Flashing an identification badge, he told her that he was an ex-police detective and had been alerted by Brandon about the reported kidnapping and the ransom demand. He said that Brandon had called him from her apartment yesterday. He further informed her that they both had been under his surveillance since that time.

Brandon had returned to the office twenty minutes later, to confirm all that Sash didn't want to believe. Brandon had betrayed her. He had strung her along, engaged in deception and trickery all this time, and most important of all had been willing to sacrifice her brother's life while doing so. She felt defeated, yet still defiant.

The three of them had been in this room for more than two hours. At first she had made desperate pleas for Brandon to follow-up on the telephone call that had come to his office. It was from a woman calling from the city of Richmond, in the San Francisco Bay area. The woman claimed to have Sweet with her, and she proved it. But Brandon had ignored her entreaties and had ordered John to continue to interrogate her. Angry and frustrated, Sash had shut down, refusing to answer any questions.

"Ms. Adams, so far everything that you've told Brandon about yourself has checked out, and we haven't called the FBI on you yet. Our contacts in the police department have told us that the authorities in Santa Cruz found the house in which you claim you and your brother were held. It belongs to a retired couple named Crayton. Sound familiar?" He paused and looked at Sash who continued to look through him. "They're on a cruise and more than likely unaware that their house has been broken into. Downstairs there were signs of the struggle you described and there was blood, but there was no sign of a body." John paused again, waiting for Sash's reaction. There was none. He sighed. "Ms. Adams, we know that you do have a five-year-old brother named Trent. Your mother and stepfather adopted him and . . . "

"Adopted?" Brandon's startled inquiry caught the attention of both John and Sash. He had been sitting in a corner of the room during the interrogation and hadn't uttered a word. It bothered him that Sash refused to acknowledge him. He had not been unmoved by her earlier entreaties to follow-up on the so called "lead" from Richmond; but some hard choices had to be made. The wild goose chase was over. Her call to him in the park had been the last straw. He had to discern truth from fiction and right now only one truth was clear. There was a child missing. The boy had to be found and time was running out. John's expertise was needed in this matter, but this latest revelation was a surprise.

"You didn't tell me that the boy was adopted." Brandon addressed John.

"I just received that information from my sources this morning. It's not in the report. We're still gathering the details."

Brandon turned his attention to Sash who continued to shut out both men. He suspected that she hated him now, and the thought disturbed him. He didn't want to care about how she felt about him. It shouldn't matter, but it did. The simple fact was that he was attracted to Sash Adams. It was something he couldn't explain and shouldn't be happening. After all, she was a stranger and possibly a criminal. He couldn't afford attaching such emotions to her. He had to focus on what was of immediate concern—a little boy whom he had never met but who had become increasingly important to him. He turned back to John.

"Do you mind leaving Sash and me alone for a few minutes."

John nodded and left the room. Sash sat as still as a statue trying to control her rage. If she didn't have a word to say to his goon she certainly had nothing to say to Brandon Plaine!

Determined not to look at him, she continued to stare ahead. Behind her she heard him rifle through a sheaf of papers that John Nathan had given him earlier. She had no doubt that it was a report on her.

After completing his task, Brandon moved to face Sash. Reaching the chair in which John had been sitting, he picked it up, turned it around and straddled it. He was sitting as close to Sash as John had been. Sash still didn't acknowledge his presence.

Brandon tossed the papers on the conference table. "I know that you hate me right now, Sash, but from the little I've read about you, " he indicated the papers on the table, "and from what I've learned about you personally, I also know that you love your brother. You've made sacrifices to make sure that he's had a home and a sense of stability after your parents died. You quit law school for a while and worked to prove that you were financially capable of being his guardian, then you resumed law school with a full course load and a child to raise and no family to support you. That had to be difficult. I have no doubt that you love that boy. "

Brandon made a move to touch Sash but she recoiled and snatched away from him with such force that her chair nearly toppled over. He reached for her to keep her from falling and she leaped from the chair. It fell to the hardwood floor with a clatter.

Startled by her reaction, Brandon looked from the fallen chair to Sash. She stood looking at him, breathing heavily, her nostrils flaring.

"Don't you *ever* put your hands on me again!" Her look was scathing.

The door to the conference room flung open and John stood in the doorway. He looked alarmed as his eyes traveled around the room finally resting on Brandon. "Is everything all right? I heard a noise."

"Yes, John, everything's fine, thank you." Brandon's eyes never left Sash.

John closed the door behind him. Brandon stood, retrieved the fallen chair and placed it upright, then turned to face Sash. His calm demeanor defied her enraged one.

"I know that you no longer trust me, but I swear to you that I'm not oblivious to the danger that your brother is in, but I'm in a no win situation here. If something happens to that boy—" Brandon paused, unable to express the guilt he would feel if the worse imaginable happened. He took a deep breath. "Believe me, I'm trying to help save his life whether you think its true or not. Expertise is needed to get your brother back; expertise that neither one of us has." Sash turned her back on him. Brandon kept talking.

"I am a man of power and influence, Sash, but I'm just a man." Brandon started to touch Sash's shoulders, thought better of it and stepped around to face her. Again, she turned away from him. He kept talking.

"I've got to tell you that this thing scares me to death. I didn't ask to have a human life in my hands. I have no power over that. I have no control over that, and I don't know what to do. I don't want to be responsible for a child's death. How could I live with myself knowing that I helped harm a child?" Brandon stepped away from Sash the impact of his own words hitting him. His stomach knotted at the reality of those words. He sank into the nearest chair. All of the emotion that had been building during these tumultuous hours hit him full force. His voice quivered as he took a shaky breath and ran his hand over his face. "I can't do the wrong thing, Sash. I can't have this boy's blood on my hands."

Sash stood looking down at Brandon in this moment of vulnerability and for the first time since she had been brought to this room for questioning she wasn't sure what to think. Was this one of his tricks? He had been a rock through this entire ordeal. It was hard to believe that Brandon Plaine would be frightened by anything. Yet, here he was confessing to being afraid. No, not simply afraid but terrified. Could this be true? If so, she might be forced to view him in a different light.

From the beginning Brandon had been a means to an end for her. He was the financial resource that would assure Sweet's return. She had counted on Brandon. His philanthropy solidified his commitment to good. She expected feelings from him of concern, guilt, even anger at the manipulation of his life by nameless forces over Sweet's desperate situation, but this man's fear wasn't something she had thought about. She had rationalized that power and influence resulted in arrogance and came without fear, but if she were to believe Brandon's words, they rendered that rationale false. This was an unexpected development and she wasn't sure how to handle it. Was this a ploy to get her to make some false confession? If it wasn't, it appeared that there were three innocent victims in this jigsaw puzzle and fear was an unwanted companion for them all.

Sash tried not to be moved by Brandon's words. He had deceived her once. He could forget her ever taking the chance on trusting him again. She closed her eyes against the possibility of repeated deceit and Sweet's face floated into vision. No matter the obstacles Brandon presented, her brother was alive. She had spoken to him. Precious hours had already been wasted and she couldn't afford to waste one more minute, no matter what she was feeling toward Brandon. She turned hostile eyes toward him.

"What would it take for you to let me go so that I can go to Richmond and get my brother?"

Surprised by the change in Sash's demeanor, Brandon wasted no words. "It would take your answering some questions."

"About what?"

"Sweet's adoption."

Sash looked perplexed. "What kind of questions?"

"Do you know where he's from? Anything about him?"

Sash's jaw tightened. "Does the child's pedigree have to be declared before you pay the ransom?"

Brandon gave her a hard stare. "I won't dignify that with an answer."

"I'm sure you won't." Her stare was just as hard. She sat in reflective silence for a moment before continuing. "Actually, I don't think this is really any of your business, but if it will get me what I want… I know all about Sweet's adoption. Sweet is my brother, but he's also my nephew."

Brandon's brows lifted in surprise. "Your nephew?"

"My step-nephew. He's my stepsister's son. The one who died."

"What was your stepsister's name?"

"Her name was Shirley."

"Shirley." Brandon echoed. His respiration increased. "Shirley Curry?"

Sash shook her head, remembering the sad saga of her stepsister's life and death. She returned to the chair he had sat upright and sank down heavily. "No, she didn't go by the last name of Curry. She went by her mother's maiden name, Matthews, even though she was married."

"And what was her married name?"

"It was Raymond. Now why are you asking?" Sash's eyes narrowed suspiciously.

Brandon looked at her steadily. "I'm trying to see where all of this fits into the picture."

Sash cut her eyes at him. "Well, Sweet is not some child whose past we knew nothing about. He's family, so his adoption is irrelevant."

* * *

Brandon managed to make a smooth exit from the conference room and back to his office without making Sash suspicious of his motives, but once the door to his office was shut behind him the information she had revealed almost brought him to his knees. Barely making it to his desk, he fell into the comfort of his father's old swivel chair. Burying his head in both hands the torrent of emotions was overwhelming.

Sash Adams' words had given him the connection. Now everything about what was happening made sense. The boy was Shirley's child! Which meant that the child also belonged to... Damn! How could this happen? Why had this happened? The past had come back to haunt him and with devastating force.

CHAPTER 10

"You can sit there and ignore me if you want, Sash, but we're in this thing together and we can't afford all of this tension between us if we're going to pull this off."

Brandon glanced at the angry woman sitting in the car beside him. They had flown to San Francisco in his private plane, and were now driving to their destination in Richmond. Sash had not said one word to him during the entire trip.

He had made the decision to listen to Sash's entreaties and follow-up on the telephone call she had received from the woman who had told her to come to Richmond. They were now twenty minutes from their destination and although he tried to ignore it, her hostile silence was getting to him.

"You know Sweet's voice when you hear it and if you're as certain that it was him as you say you are then this may be it. We can get your brother back. So why don't you drop all of this hostility for a while and let's work together to save him. You can hate me again later. The precautions that John and I are taking now are necessary. We must have the

FBI involved. I should have done that in the beginning. It's safer this way." He paused, hoping for a reply. This was the most exasperating woman! "Come on, Sash, give me a break here! I'm doing what I have to do to save Sweet. Whether you agree or not, I'm trying to get him home alive the best way I can. And not once have you said thank you for the effort."

Sash weighed Brandon's words carefully. She never would forgive this man for his blatant betrayal. His sudden decision to listen to her about the call she received from Richmond didn't make up for what he did to her. She had begun to trust Brandon but he had never trusted her at all. The kidnappers had been explicit about the authorities not being involved, but now they were involved and she was frightened. Brandon was wired. The authorities were trailing them. Where would this all lead? For Brandon it was about the money and damn the consequences of his actions. Sweet was nothing to him but a name and a face in a photo. To her he was flesh and blood. To her he was love and affection. Sweet was all she had, and she had vowed to do whatever it took to save him even if it meant working with this traitor. FBI or not, the two of them had a job to finish and when she had Sweet back, she would say thank you and good-bye to Mr. Brandon Plaine. Sash shifted in her seat and looked at him.

"Tell me something, was there ever one minute that we've been together through all of this that you ever trusted me? Have you ever trusted *anybody*?"

Her last words were spat at him and their impact was powerful. Brandon wanted to spit back at her that trust only brought heartache. He knew that for a fact. Right now she was hurt and angry and she probably wouldn't believe anything he told her. She sure wouldn't believe that he *had* began to believe her incredible story, that he regretted having to deceive her and that he was even beginning to care about her. So he said, "Sash, I did what I thought was best."

"If you call lies and deceit *best* I guess you're right." Sash sighed. "I shouldn't have been surprised that this has happened. You gave me plenty of warnings, but I chose to ignore them. Tell me something, was it all staged?"

"Nothing was staged, Sash. I'm a very wealthy man and prey for any jackal out there who thinks that I might be easy game. All I was doing was protecting myself.

"And forget about my brother."

"No, he was always on my mind. Trying to find out what's happened to him has been one of the things that has kept me involved in all this. It's true that I had called John by the time we went to the bank, because I still wasn't certain about your story . . ."

"Then why the telephone call to the bank president? Why get the money?"

"I figured that I'd better have the money ready just in case I needed it, but I *was* aware that the bank did close early that day. When we got there I wanted to see what you would say or do if it looked like I couldn't get the ransom."

"I assume that I passed your sick test."

"Let's say that sometimes you've been quite convincing and other times you haven't. You're an enigma, Sash. I've never met anyone like you. You're a handful that's for sure. This whole thing had been a major challenge to my ego."

"I wish." Sash rolled her eyes preferring to look out of

the window than at him. "I don't think there's any wind strong enough to blow your ego away."

Brandon chuckled. "Lady, you are truly humbling."

"You don't know how to spell the word. This is a big joke to you, something to occupy your idle time. I'm just a pawn in your little chess game. So I don't understand why you're continuing with this farce. If you don't trust me or believe me then why are we going to Richmond? Why the sudden about face? It's obvious that your lackey thinks that I'm this terrible person trying to lure you into some trap when we get there."

"Well, you've got to admit that this telephone call did come out of nowhere at a very convenient time. While I'm making the ransom drop, your brother suddenly appears somewhere else. Come on now."

"I can't explain the circumstances. I'm only the messenger. I told you and your flunky, I don't know how these people got your private numbers! I don't know how this woman is involved! I never saw or heard a woman. All I know is that I talked to Sweet and she told me that if I wanted him back I had to come to Richmond. My brother is alive and that's all I care about!"

Brandon glanced at her. He hated the way things were, but there were so many unanswered questions that there wasn't much he could do to make the situation better for now. This trip to Richmond could mean that some of those questions would eventually be answered. Maybe after that things might improve, then maybe not. He tried to lighten the mood.

"You know something, Sash, everything that's happened these past few hours hasn't been a farce. I really enjoyed last night—especially the dance."

Sash slid narrowed eyes his way, "Yeah? I'm glad at least *one* of us did."

Brandon shook his head at her stubborn resistance. "Oh, I think you enjoyed it too," he teased. "You just don't want to admit it that's all."

"Then so be it, Brandon, you're right. But of course you're *always* right. So you must be right about my enjoying the dance and being chased through the streets by your lackey and making me think that we were being followed. You ought to be a director instead of a CEO. Between the race to the bank and that phony chase scene after we left the dance, you could win an Oscar."

Brandon stared ahead as he recalled both events. "Sash, there's something you should know. It's true that my man, John, has been on the case keeping tabs on what's been going on, and I was aware of being followed by my security team at the drop site, but I did think that it was the kidnappers following us last night in the limo. Whether you believe me or not, it wasn't staged, and I've got a feeling that today might be just as harrowing. I'm not looking forward to it."

He pulled up to the telephone booth in Richmond where the caller had stated that the next contact would be made. According to the woman, this call would reveal where Sweet could be picked up.

"This is it." Brandon gazed past Sash at the neat little houses beyond the corner on which the telephone booth stood. The neighborhood appeared to be residential and working class. There was a small mom and pop store across the street from the telephone booth. He could see children playing farther up the street. Other than that there appeared to be no other signs of life. Yet, Brandon felt a sense of relief knowing that the authorities were around somewhere, watching.

Sash examined their surroundings as well, wondering if their next step might be a mistake. "Are you sure this is it?" She nodded toward the solitary telephone booth.

Brandon looked at the sign perched above the street on a nearby pole. "It's the right street."

Nervously, Sash chewed on her bottom lip. Was this a trap? She wished she knew. She glanced at the clock on the dashboard. They were ten minutes late for the call. If Brandon had only listened to her earlier! She exhaled slowly, forcing down the rage rising within her, then whispered, "I pray that she'll call back."

Brandon sensed that she hadn't meant to say the words aloud, but the hitch in her voice reflected both her fear and her anger toward him. In those words were an unspoken accusation that it was his fault that they were late and may have missed the call. Well, she was right, but he couldn't do much about that now. He would just add this grievance to the many on her list against him.

"Tell me again exactly what the woman said." He knew that the request was redundant, but he didn't know what else to say.

Sash repeated what she had told him numerous times before. "She said that if I came here to Richmond to this telephone booth, she would call and tell me where to pick up Sweet."

"And she didn't mention the ransom money?" If he sounded skeptical he was.

"I told you, no! She put Sweet on the phone. He begged me to come after him and..."

"How did he sound?"

The anxious tone in Brandon's voice drew Sash's attention. This was the first time she'd heard it.

"He sounded scared. But she said that he was fine physically, just a little dehydrated."

"Dehydrated." Brandon repeated absently. "That's an interesting observation. You didn't say that before. Did she say anything else you didn't mention? Anything at all?"

Sash gave an exasperated sigh. "She said that she was giving him fluids and that he'd be fine."

Brandon cocked a brow. "Fluids? She said fluids?"

"Yes, *fluids*, Brandon. Like water? Juice?" Sash dropped her head in her hand and wished that the man would disappear, but he seemed excited by her revelation.

"I know, but don't you think that's a strange way to put it?"

She was about to answer and tell him who she thought was *really* strange when the telephone in the booth rang. Neither of them reacted. It rang a second time. They scrambled from the car. Sash squeezed into the booth while Brandon stood outside. Eagerly, Sash answered the call. Brandon listened.

"Hello! Hello! This is Sash Adams."

"Did you bring the police with you?" The voice on the other end was soft, tearful and frightened.

Sash glanced at Brandon. "No, I didn't, but Brandon Plaine is with me."

"I'm glad to hear that Ms. Adams. I'm real glad."

Sash reeled back from the telephone. Alarmed, Brandon grabbed the receiver.

"Hello! This is Brandon Plaine. What's going on?"

The voice that greeted him wasn't female. It was male. It

was a voice with which he had become all too familiar in the past hours. Brandon muttered an expletive. It was a trap!

"Well, if it ain't the great Mr. Plaine himself. I know you're feeling good about playing the hero to the little lady, but we both know why you're really sticking around, don't we? Questions. Lots of questions. But you know what? Not one of them is gonna be answered, because of you and that smart aleck broad, to say nothing of this…this…" The sound of someone being slapped could be heard in the background followed by a woman's painful squeal. He addressed Brandon again. "I had to follow you two all over the city trying to find this double crossing, two timing…" He was interrupted again, this time by a crying child.

Sash snatched the phone from Brandon's hand. "We brought the money, you freak, and if you touch a hair on my brother's head you won't get a dime of it!" She had recovered from the shock of hearing the voice of the man she had grown to despise and now she was hopping mad. Brandon squeezed next to Sash so that they could share the phone receiver.

The kidnapper railed. "You must think I'm a fool, lady! This is a set up! "

"Do you want the money or not?" Brandon snarled, baiting the hook.

"You're telling me that you brought the money with you and didn't even know I was here. I knew it!" He turned from the receiver to address the woman. "You *were* double crossing me. You ran with this kid to get the money yourself! Tell me another lie!"

"No! No!" Sash intervened. "She didn't ask for the ransom money."

"Do you think I'm crazy? This is some kind of trick."

"No! It's not a trick," Sash reassured him. "Like I said, we did bring the money. We didn't know whether this phone call was another way to get it or not. So it made sense to bring it just in case. Now where's my brother? Let me speak to him."

There was momentary silence on the other end, then, "Oh you must be ready to hear the gun shot, lady, I know you two brought the cops with you..."

"No!" Sash lied, trying not to panic. "There are no cops."

"Then why are you late? Is this phone tapped? This call is being traced ain't it?"

"How?" She lied again. "It's a phone booth! We just got here. We had to fly all the way from Monterey." Her heart was pounding out of her chest.

There was a pause then, "Stay where you are. I'll call back."

Brandon and Sash looked at each other quizzically at the sound of the dial tone. Sash was the first to speak.

"Why did he hang up? I don't understand?"

The distress in her voice lead Brandon to grasp at any straw that he could to soothe her. "He's scared of being set up. He must be moving some place else to call."

His assumption proved true. A short while later the authorities called him on his cell phone and reported that they had traced the call to a telephone booth in downtown Richmond. It was empty when they got there. The hope was that another call would be forthcoming. All they could do now was wait.

For what seemed like hours, Sash and Brandon hovered around the telephone booth waiting for the promised return call. She was nearly paralyzed with fear as she prayed with every minute that passed that Brandon's having involved the authorities wouldn't cost her brother his life. Thirty minutes had passed when the telephone rang again. Sash nearly tore the receiver off its cradle.

The abductor picked up the conversation as if it had never been interrupted. "Put Plaine back on the line."

"I'm here," Brandon's tone was as cold as that of the man on the other end. "But we don't have another thing to say to each other until we talk to the boy."

There was a rustling on the other end, some muted whispers and then the sound of a small, quivering voice, "Hello."

At the sound of Sweet's voice Sash fought to maintain control. "Hi, Sweety. Are you okay?"

"Sash! Sash! Come get me! Please!" His anguished plea was heartbreaking. Sash clamped her hand over her mouth to keep from crying out. Gently, Brandon held her to him lending her his strength. The animosity between them was temporarily forgotten.

"We'll see each other soon, baby," she managed to choke.

The sinister voice replaced the innocent one. "You and Mr. Moneybags had better listen closely, because I'm not gonna repeat myself."

He wasted no time giving them instructions for the new ransom site before the line went dead. After the disconnect Sash stood in the tiny space with her heart palpitating. She could barely breathe. All she could think about was the sound of Sweet's voice. He was alive and come hell or high water she was bringing him home.

CHAPTER 11

The latest drop was at midnight. At 11:30 Brandon pulled up to the designated site, a nondescript playground in a desolated part of town long forgotten by the city. The instructions had been precise. Like before, the money was to be put into plain shopping bags and the bags were to be dropped into a trash can marked #9 located on the playground. This time Sash was to accompany Brandon and they were ordered to come alone. If one cop was spotted, they were told that it would mean Sweet's life. The call from the abductor had been traced to another telephone booth, but he was gone by the time the authorities arrive. So now Brandon and Sash found themselves in what could be the final chapter of this saga and it could prove to be the most dangerous one of all.

Brandon looked at Sash huddled against the door. She was praying. If there ever was a woman with more strength than this one he hadn't met her. Her emotional dam had almost burst a few times but her faith seemed as strong as her resolve. He admired her. She was not only strong and confident, but also undeniably audacious. His initial doubts about her had all but faded. Maybe one day she would come to understand that John's involvement in this drama had been necessary not only for his well being but for hers, too. He wanted her to forgive his deception. He wanted her to need him, and not only for his money.

The skepticism, doubts, suspicions and betrayal remained barriers between them; but surely they could be overcome. That is, if they got the opportunity, because what they faced this evening was real, as real as his growing feelings for Sash. Despite the assurance of the authorities who monitored their movements, what they were doing was dangerous, and Brandon found a fierce need to protect Sash.

"What are you thinking?"

Sash's voice jolted Brandon out of his contemplation. It was unexpected. She had continued to give him the silent treatment after they received the telephone call. He knew that she was still angry at the way he had handled things, but if she was willing to open the door she had closed he was more than willing to step through it.

"I was thinking about how you nearly bit my head off earlier when I asked you not to come here with me."

Sash stiffened. After the last telephone call, he had the nerve to tell her that he was going to the meeting place alone or with a decoy, despite the kidnapper's instructions. The verbal argument had been long and loud. The authorities had to intervene; but nobody was able to talk her out of accompanying him.

Sash's eyes narrowed as she recalled their earlier altercation. "You didn't *ask* me not to come, Brandon, you *ordered* me."

"Well, I..."

"Well I nothing! There was no way that I was going to let

you come out here and make this drop without me. This is my life and Sweet's life, not yours. You don't have the right to make decisions for either one of us!"

"I don't have the right? You've got to be kidding! A stranger snatched a five-year-old boy and a hardheaded woman off the street and demanded money from *me*!" He pointed to himself. "That gave me the right!"

Sash's nostrils flared in indignation. "Oh, so you're worried about your precious money? That's it! You don't want to lose your money. Well, don't concern yourself, because I can assure you that if you lose your precious ransom money if it takes me the rest of my life, you'll get back every dime. I promise you that."

Brandon was seething. "The money? Do you think I care about the money? I've got plenty of money. It means nothing to me." Brandon grabbed Sash by the shoulders. "You little fool! Don't you realize that what we're doing is dangerous? Don't you realize that what we're doing could get both of us killed? The money is the last thing on my mind now. It's you I'm worried about! It's you I care about! It's you who I want to stay alive!"

Brandon's lips descended on Sash like a fiery branding iron—hot, sizzling. He overwhelmed her senses deepening the kiss as he drew her closer to him, tasting her, savoring her, reveling in the feelings he was experiencing having her in his arms. He moaned his pleasure and she responded.

Sash couldn't seem to help herself. Brandon's touch made her body spring to life. The rational process of thought no longer controlled her actions. Instead, her body took its own lead, disconnected from reality by the pleasure it now enjoyed. Her arms slid around Brandon's neck. His hand slid with purpose to her breast, and lingered. His mouth bruised her mouth in suppressed passion. She responded. Oblivious to the console, they straddled it, frustrated by the obstacle standing between them and complete surrender. But gradually reasoning returned.

It happened slowly as they untangled legs and arms and each retreated to their side of the car. With shaking hands, Sash smoothed her mussed hair and straightened her clothing, angry with herself, angry with Brandon and embarrassed beyond belief. How could she let this happen? She hated this man. He was working with the authorities. The man was jeopardizing Sweet. She could not be attracted to Brandon. She would *not* be attracted to him.

With shaking hands, Brandon ran his hands over his face. How could he let this happen? He had not intended to let her know what he was beginning to feel for her, certainly not here and certainly not now. What in the hell had happened? He felt shell-shocked. "I…I'm sorry, Sash. I didn't mean for that to happen."

"No! It shouldn't have happened. I told you not to touch me and I meant it. I mean, you don't trust me and after all that's happen with Sweet…"

"I…I…know. What I did was despicable. You're vulnerable, and I took advantage of that…"

"Yes, you did. Just because we've been through a lot together…"

"You're right and with all of this tension…"

"Yes, the tension." Sash covered her eyes in dismay. "This whole thing has made me crazy. I just want it over with. I just want to get Sweet back." Uncovering her eyes she looked at Brandon for a moment, then wide-eyed, she whispered frantically, "Could they hear what we were doing over that wire?"

Brandon wanted to laugh out loud at the look on her face. He also wanted to hold her, comfort her and reassure that everything would be all right; but he knew that if he touched her again it would surely reignite the passion they both found best to deny. Instead, he gave her his standard, "Don't worry about it." Then he turned his thoughts to how to protect her. It was too dangerous for Sash to be here.

It was true that the FBI agents were trailing them, but Sash had refused a wire. They had no way to monitor her outside of this car unless she was with him. The authorities had assured him that they would be in close contact with them during this entire ordeal, but Brandon had taken steps to help himself. The agents didn't know that he carried a gun tucked beneath his jacket. He had carried it earlier when he went to the park and felt it even more important that he carry it with him now. If there was trouble, he was ready.

Staring out the front windshield Brandon surveyed the neighborhood. This area of Richmond bore all the scars of urban decay. There were entire square blocks of weed infested lots, interrupted here and there by dilapidated houses, some of which had been long abandoned. The evening was chilly and neighbors who might have spent warmer nights visiting on cracked front stoops, now huddled inside. Occasionally, a house filled with life would stand among the ruins. Laughter drifted from the barred windows and latched security doors of the few houses nearby, but most of the landscape around the playground was desolate, with waist high weeds and grass that would allow anyone to hide undetected, including the kidnapper.

Brandon needed to put distance between him and Sash, for reasons other than the heat that still lingered between them. If things went badly with the ransom drop, he wanted to make sure that she was as far away as possible.

"I'm going to move closer to the playground," he informed her as he slid out of the car. He ignored her attempt to protest. Opening the back door, he withdrew the shopping bags containing the money then walked around to Sash's window. He knocked on it and she rolled it down just as he withdrew a set of walkie-talkies from one of the bags. He put one in her hand. Sash looked surprised.

"What's this for?"

"For you. You wouldn't take a wire from the agents but I'm asking you to take this so that you can keep in touch with me. I also want you to slide into the driver's seat. I left the key in the ignition. At the first sign of trouble you drive away like a bat out of hell." With that he walked away.

"Brandon! Wait!" Sash called from the open window, panicked at the thought that he was changing the instructions. He wasn't to get out of the car until time for the drop. Despite the authorities covering them, anything could happen to him. The thought upset Sash as he ignored her call to him and kept walking. Sash pounded in frustration on the padded dashboard. The man got on her last nerve! It was as obvious as the nose on her face what he was doing. He was putting distance between them in an effort to protect her, and she resented it. She told him more than once that she could take care of herself and she could.

Rolling the window up, she opened her shoulder bag, unzipped the center pouch and withdrew a small handgun. It was Brandon's. She had discovered it in a hiding place on his plane on their way here. He had yet to miss it. She wasn't an expert on guns, but she knew enough to release the safety, point and shoot. If it became necessary, she planned on doing just that.

She looked up to see how far Brandon had progressed in his trek into the darkness. The street was empty. He was no longer there. Sash frowned. How had he vanished so quickly? She pushed the button on the walkie-talkie and whispered.

"Brandon! Brandon! Where are you?"

There was no response. Sash swallowed nervously as she peered past the windshield into the darkness. The bark of a dog and the sound of an ambulance siren in the distance interrupted the silence of the night; but there was still no sign of Brandon. Where *was* he?

"Brandon, I know you hear me." The whisper was louder this time, more urgent. "I can't see you. Where are you?"

Sash stopped short, alerted by a sound. She could hear the crunching of tires against the pavement. She lowered the window a crack and listened intently. The crunching sound drew closer. Glancing in the rear view mirror she spotted the headlights of the car approaching from behind. Was this them? She glanced at the illuminated numbers on the dashboard. It was 11:50. It could be them, but it was still early. Brandon hadn't made the drop yet. As the car drew closer she lay across the front seat to conceal her presence. As she did so, Brandon broke his silence. His voice was calm.

"Sash, did you hear that? What is it?"

"A car is coming," she responded excitedly.

"Is it them?"

"I don't know."

Sash raised her head enough to see if she could see the car and its driver. The passing car had tinted windows.

"I don't think it's them. It's a little too early."

Sash could hear the hum of the engine as the car slowly passed by. Then, waiting until she could no longer hear the idle of the engine, she eased up cautiously. Once again it was quiet. She informed Brandon.

"The car passed by. I don't see it." Sitting up completely, Sash glanced at the dashboard clock. It was nearly midnight. I don't know why you got out of the car so early, but now it's time for the drop."

She looked out the front windshield. Less than a second later a figure suddenly appeared in the distance and crossed the street. It was Brandon. He moved swiftly toward the playground with a shopping bag in each hand. A single light illuminated the playground and the basketball court. Brandon's tall figure looked shadowy and mysterious as he moved with purpose through the night. Sash watched as he walked across the matted grass toward an aged jungle gym. Stopping at a wire trashcan he examined it closely, then headed toward the basketball court.

She needed to get closer to Brandon so that she could... Could what? Help him? Protect him? She would if it came to that. There was no sign of the FBI agents who were supposed to be protecting them. Where were they anyway? Could she and Brandon really count on them?

Hurriedly slipping the walkie-talkie into one jean pocket and the gun into another, Sash opened the door and slid out, never noticing the walkie-talkie fall from her pocket to the ground. She did notice the scattering of cars parked on the street. Aware that the kidnapper may be watching from anywhere, Sash used the cars as cover as she scurried up the street closer to the playground.

Sash was moving forward quickly when she was distracted by a noise behind her. Turning, she saw a car with the headlights off moving slowly down the street. Ducking behind a nearby bush, she watched it moving forward. Sash recognized the car and its tinted windows. It was the car that had driven down the street once before. She froze. It was the abductors. She was sure of it.

Her attention returned to the playground. Brandon was near the basketball court walking away from a second wire trash can. His hands were empty. He had found the drop site.

Sash reached for the walkie-talkie to signal Brandon that their nemesis was here. Her pocket was empty. There was no way for her to communicate with him. Frantically, Sash's eyes searched the ground in the dark in an effort to spot the walkie talkie that could prove to be her lifeline. She couldn't find it. Her attention returned to Brandon who never broke stride.

Just as Brandon crossed the street, increasing the distance between him and the playground, the car picked up speed. The monotonous hum of its engine became a roar and with tires squealing the car swerved across the dividing line of the small, two-way street and onto the curb outside the gateless fence leading into the playground.

Caught off guard by the escalation in activity, Brandon whirled around in time to see someone fling the passenger car door open, leap from the vehicle and head straight to the wastebasket he had just left. The figure was short, dressed in jeans and a hooded sweatshirt. The figure's trot turned into a full run as the bounty from the trash can was retrieved. Burdened by the weight of the bags the figure headed back toward the car.

From the back of the car came a child's piercing cry. Still crouched in the safety of her hiding place Sash watched the action impassively until jolted by the sound of the cry. It was Sweet! She'd know his cry anywhere. The cry was pain filled and it brought her instantly to her feet. No longer shielded by the security of her hiding place, Sash withdrew the gun. Safety was no longer a consideration. She had one goal and one goal only as she started down the street, running. She was going to get her brother and she dared anyone to stop her.

CHAPTER 12

Brandon also heard the child's plaintive cries, but unlike Sash, his close proximity to the idling car allowed him to hear the slap that had preceded the cry. Brandon had retreated into the shelter of the thicket of bushes across the street from the playground in which he had been hiding prior to having made the drop. He wasn't sure whether the kidnapper had observed his retreat, but he was close enough to see and to hear all of the action. What he heard made his blood boil. Brandon's hand settled on the gun resting in his jacket pocket. He was determined to use it if he had to and from the sounds coming from the car he might be forced to do just that. It took a coward to attack a frightened child. He could only hope that he would get the opportunity to get his hands on the bully.

Tearing his attention from the car back to the playground he watched as the hooded figure reached the car. Brandon guessed by the figure's movements that it was a woman. He had no doubt that it was the woman caller. She was at the car and Brandon waited anxiously for the young boy to emerge from the car. The abductors had the money, or at least they thought that they had it. If prayers were answered Sweet would be free before they discovered what they really had were marked bills with a tracking device hidden among them. The child's only hope for life was to be released here and now. Brandon watched with baited breath willing the boy to appear.

The woman had reached the car. Shoving the bags through the open window to the driver, she scurried around the back of the car to the passenger side. She was reaching for the door handle when her attention was diverted. She hesitated.

Following her gaze, Brandon saw what had drawn her attention. His heart nearly stopped. Sash was moving down the sidewalk in plain sight and she was moving fast. He summarized that she had heard Sweet's cry and that all rationale had been abandoned. As he watched her racing down the street he frantically called into the wire asking the authorities for help. Feeling less than confident in the reassurance that they would come to their rescue in time, it was at that moment that Brandon make a split second decision that would mean either life or death. Withdrawing the gun from his pocket, his focus switched back to the woman at the car; but he found that she was having problems of her own.

The woman was pulling on the car door handle of the passenger side, but the driver had stepped on the gas and was moving away from the curb. The car was rapidly picking up speed as she trotted along beside it calling to the driver to stop. She was being ignored. As the car's speed continued to escalate, the back door opened a crack and a small figure appeared in the shadows of the car's interior. Brandon gasped. It was Sweet. He almost screamed out his name. It was clear that the boy was about to make his escape when the woman managed to open the back door completely and dived into the car. Both woman and boy tumbled inside the car's interior as the car door dangled open precariously by the hinges. Suddenly, with tires screeching, the driver made a U-turn, heading back in Sash's direction.

Emerging from his hiding place, gun in hand, Brandon followed the fleeing vehicle at a gallop. Grappling for his walkie-talkie as he did so, he yelled into it.

"Sash, here they come! Here they come! Get out of the way! Get out of the way!" There was no response.

Sash observed the action ahead of her. She could see Brandon talking into the walkie-talkie but her mind was focused on only one scenario, releasing Sweet from his captors. Her only concern was that the kidnappers still had Sweet and that they were getting away. That wasn't going to happen.

As the lights turned in her direction, Sash found refuge behind an abandoned car. Tightening her grip on the handle of the gun, she watched the car approach. A dim street light in the middle of the block provided her with the light she would need to assure her of hitting her target. There would be only seconds to take aim and stop the car and chances were slim that could be accomplished, but she had to try. With adrenaline pumping she scurried around the front of the car and settled into a crouch. Whispering a quick prayer for Sweet's safety she held the gun with both hands, pointed it and took aim at the car's front tire.

The car was only a few feet away. The streetlight reflected off the car's tinted windshield and Sash could only guess at the face of the man sitting behind the steering wheel. She wasn't sure that he saw her, but if he did she could imagine his taunting laugh at having extorted the money from Brandon. Well, she would have the last laugh after she stopped the car and she *was* going to stop it.

Every muscle in Sash's body was tense. The hatred she felt for her faceless nemesis welled up inside her like bile. The car was within sight. *Shoot!* The word exploded inside her head as loudly as the shot that echoed in the night.

Lights flickered on in nearby houses and people peered from behind drawn curtains and shades to see what had disturbed their peace. Further down the street, Brandon stood, gun in hand, also aiming at the fleeing vehicle. His shot had also pierced the stillness of the night and had hit its intended target—one of the car's back tires. Simultaneously, Sash's shot hit one of the front tires. Both tires ruptured with a loud pop. A child's terrified screams came from the car's interior.

A hubcap from one of the tires jumped from its mounting and rolled around in a grotesque circle dance before landing in the street with a clang. Crippled by flat tires at a fast speed the car jerked out of control. It jumped the curb, careening through waist high weeds and grass that covered the vacant lot next to the playground. Sash sprinted after the car, calling for Sweet. Brandon did the same, calling her name. Fighting tangled weeds that lashed at her hands and legs, Sash reached the lot before Brandon and was the first to see the large tree rising majestically above its untended domain. She made no connection to its towering beauty and disaster. Her only goal was to reach Sweet. She was within yards of her destination when she heard the dull crush of metal then smelled the sweet odor of gasoline.

Whether it was the kidnapper's scream, Sweet's screams or her own that rang out as the car exploded was unclear, but Sash's lungs ached with the sound of her brother's name as she rushed toward the fury of crackling flames that followed. She beat at the weeds that stood between her and the car as she drew closer, so close that she could feel the searing heat of the flames that lit the midnight sky. She was almost there, a few feet away from saving Sweet, and then suddenly she was tackled. Sash fell face first to the ground.

Brandon was holding her, dragging her away from the wreckage. She fought him, twisting, squirming, wiggling, and struggling to break free as she screamed for Sweet. She screamed his name over and over.

The light of the flames bore witness to the agony unleashed from them both as they struggled in the shadow of the fire. The force of the collision had demolished the vehicle, leaving only the opened back door on the passenger side hanging by a hinge, unscathed. The subsequent explosion had extinguished any hope of survival for the car's occupants. There were no signs of life. But any hope was better than no hope and somehow Sash slipped from Brandon's grasp. She started once again toward the flames.

The heat was intense and Sash shielded her face with one arm as she advanced on the burning hulk. Her screams intermingled with gut wrenching sobs as she stood before her brother's funeral pyre—a pyre that she had helped light. The pain was unbearable as sobs tore from her throat. She tried to leap forward but Brandon caught her firmly by the waist dragging her backward in a vice like grip which she fought with matched determination. The struggle was fierce as she fought to die and he fought to keep her alive.

As their struggle continued, voices and footsteps could be heard in the distance as people ran from their homes toward the field. Revolving red lights from squad cars cast eerie shadows in the night. Someone knelt beside Sash and

Brandon asking about their welfare. Brandon didn't answer and Sash couldn't answer as she lay in his arms. Her screams had ceased and had turned into a low, mournful wail, a primal sound, like that of a wounded animal. It was over. Sweet was gone. The ruins of a vacant lot had become his burial ground.

Brandon felt Sash's pain as he buried his face in her hair, holding her close, in an attempt to shut out the sights and sounds around them. Fire engines had arrived behind the squad cars. The smell of charred remains and smoldering metal intermingled with the glare of rotating lights and the din of voices shouting commands and making inquiries. The quiet night pulsated with activity. It was alive with motion, but not for Sash and Brandon.

Immobile, Sash lay in Brandon's arm tasting her tears and feeling her pain. It was intense. Her goal, her mission had been clear, to get Sweet home safely, but she had failed. The possibility no longer existed. All hope for that had gone up in flames. Now only guilt, pain and misery remained.

As Sash began to slip into the welcomed oblivion of unconsciousness, the sounds around her began to fade, including Brandon's effort to keep her with him. *"Sash! Sash!"* Also fading into the background was the disembodied voice of authority giving orders. *"Hey, Hartman, look at this. Over here! Over here!"*

The sound of rushed movement, hushed conversation and the memory of a child's plaintive cry all faded into the distance as Sash descended into welcomed darkness.

CHAPTER 13

Sash's eyes felt as heavy as lead as she slowly opened them. The light in the room was blinding and she blinked against the intrusion as she regained consciousness.

"Sash?" It was Brandon calling her name and he sounded worried. What did he want? She looked around, but her vision was blurred. Where were they? Gradually the jumble of the day's events began to unravel in her mind, climaxing in the fiery ball of flame that had taken her brother's life.

"Sweet!" Sash screamed, sitting up with a jolt as the reality turned to grief. Sobs racked her body.

"Sash, don't." Brandon reached out to comfort her and drew back stunned as she slapped him hard across the face.

"Murderer!" Her face was contorted with hate. "You killed my brother! You called the cops! It was you! Your fault! You killed my brother!" Dropping back onto the bed, Sash covered her face with her hands, weeping uncontrollably. She didn't hear Brandon draw away from the bed, nor did she hear the door to the room open. She didn't hear the rustle of movement in the room or the muttered conversation of those around her. Sash's mind, body and soul were all consumed by the grief of her lost, so much so that she didn't hear the whispered sound of her name being called—not at first.

"Sash?" The voice grew a little louder. "Sash, please. Don't cry." It was the voice of a child. The voice belonged to Sweet.

What cruel joke was Brandon pulling? Did his cruelty and insensitivity know any bounds? Sash could barely open her swollen eyes, but she was determined to get Brandon Plaine told. Through the tears and over wrought emotions Sash forced herself to focus on the face that she could feel near her own. She was ready to attack Brandon again if necessary. She wanted him out of her life!

"Sash?" Two warm hands were placed on each of her cheeks and a small face appeared before her blurry eyes and peered down at her. "Sash, are you awake?"

Both the voice and the concerned face belonged to Sweet. Sash opened her eyes in disbelief. Was she seeing a ghost?

"Sweet?" She pushed herself up on her elbows. "Sweet? You're alive?"

The crooked grin bestowed on her confirmed that it was him. He threw his arms around Sash's neck knocking her back onto the bed. He covered her face with noisy kisses but Sash was hesitant to touch him at first, still unable to believe that he had survived the fiery crash. Slowly, in measured degrees her arms curled around his small body. She caressed him and inhaled him, touched him and checked him for bumps and bruises until her mind was ready to comprehend that a miracle had happened. Sweet was alive! She was holding him in her arms, and except for a few scrapes and bruises he seemed to be unharmed. She could hardly believe it. She had longed for this moment, prayed for it fervently. Sash's arms tightened around the little boy. She returned his noisy kisses with ones of her own as tears of joy replaced tears of despair.

"Stop Sash! You're squashing me!" Sweet protested trying to wiggle free.

Brandon stood at Sash's bedside feeling like an intruder as he watched the happy reunion. The love between the boy and his sister couldn't be denied. He felt a twinge of jealousy as he watched them. He could remember how it felt to love one person so deeply. He was happy for both Sash and the boy and he hated to be the one to break up their reunion, but...

"I'm sorry, Sash, but you've got to get some rest."

Forcing herself to tear her eyes from her brother, Sash turned her attention to Brandon. "Where are we?" For the first time she noticed her surroundings. The room she was in was richly decorated, with brocade wallpaper and expensive bedroom furnishings. There was an IV in her arm.

"We're in a private room at the hospital. The ambulance brought you here. The medic said that you were in shock. How are you feeling?"

"You sick, Sash?" Sweet's face registered his concern.

"No, sweetheart. I'm fine." Sash sat up with him still in her arms as she addressed Brandon. "I don't like hospitals. I don't want to be here."

Brandon decided not to argue. "All right, but we may have trouble trying to get out of here. It's a madhouse outside."

"There's police cars outside, Sash," Sweet said with a combination of awe and fear in his voice. "There were fires trucks and firemen, too, at the other place. Sash, do I have to talk to those people?" Sash's questioning eyes went to Brandon.

"The FBI wants to talk to him and the press is gathering. Let me get the doctor, so he can sign you out. We'll probably have to leave by some sort of back entrance. Do you think that you can make it? "

"Of course." Sash sat up on the side of the bed and found her shoes placed neatly beside it. Sliding her feet into them smoothly, she looked up at Brandon. "Go get that doctor to take this thing out of my arm. I'm ready to leave."

* * *

Surreptitiously, Brandon watched Sash as she cuddled her brother while the boy was being questioned by the FBI agents. She never ceased to amaze him. He marveled at how well she had held up over the hours since Sweet had been rescued. He knew she had to be exhausted, but she refused to rest until all matters could be settled regarding Sweet. After successfully leaving the hospital without being detected by the media, they had been hustled into a waiting car by the FBI and had taken Brandon's plane back to his Monterey home. He had called ahead to his private physician to meet them at the house. There, Brandon had insisted that Sash and Sweet be further examined. They were both declared physically fit.

Up to this point, the three of them had stayed one step ahead of the media, but Brandon knew that their luck might not last. When word leaked out that the founder of Plaine Deal Media was the target of an extortion attempt the media pressure would be intense. The FBI agreed to conduct questioning of Sweet and Sash here in his home and he could only hope that they would be safe from the media for now. He was anxious for them to get through the questioning so that the two of them could get some rest.

From the moment she regained consciousness and discovered that Sweet was alive all of Sash's attention had been focused on him. She had made sure that he was fed and got some sleep on the plane. She was anxious that the questioning the authorities insisted that Sweet undergo be over with soon. What he had endured over the past few days had been torturous. She was concerned about not only his physical health, but his mental health as well. Sweet didn't want to talk to the authorities about his experience and he did so reluctantly, but he did recount for Sash his miraculous escape from the flaming wreckage.

He recalled how the woman in the car leaped from the back door with him in her arms. They rolled onto the ground into the waist high weeds. The impact had stunned Sweet but it had knocked the woman unconscious. Her body had cushioned his from the impact of the fall. She had been seriously injured as a result and was now hospitalized and lay in a coma. Her act of selflessness had saved the child's life.

According to Sweet, it wasn't the first time that "the lady" had shielded him from harm. Sash hovered over him while he described his time with the "mean man" as one in which he lived with constant threats. But "the lady" had promised Sweet that she would protect him. She had expressed regret to him that she had been a part of the abduction and had fled with Sweet from the "mean man" even before Sash escaped from the basement in Santa Cruz. She had fled in the gray van Sash had described to Brandon.

"She told me that I would be her little boy," Sweet recalled with a frown. "But I told her I wanted to go home."

Whether the subsequent phone call that Sash had answered in Brandon's office was an attempt to comply with Sweet's request or another plan to get the money would remain a mystery until the woman awakened. Whatever the reason, her effort to flee from her partner had proved unsuccessful.

"The lady and me went to go get something to eat and that mean man found us. The lady was crying and he said he would get rid of her like he did that other man if she didn't shut up." Sweet yawned and rubbed his eyes.

Each adult in the room zeroed in on the child's mention of the disappearance of another man. The authorities gave Sash the nod to take the forefront in the questioning of the exhausted child.

"There won't be many more questions, Sweet," she said reassuring him with a kiss. "But did you see what happened to the other man?"

She was relieved when he shook his head, and snuggled closer to her, his eyelids drooping slowly over his dark brown eyes. Sash shifted him in her arms and stood.

"That's it for today, gentlemen. I've got to get my brother home and put him to bed. Could I hitch a ride home from one of you? We're both about to drop." She noticed that the agents from whom she requested a ride looked at Brandon expectantly.

Brandon licked his lips nervously. "Do you guys mind giving us a few minutes?"

The men left the room without protest seemingly oblivious to the look of confusion on Sash's face. Closing the door behind them, Brandon turned to Sash.

"What's up?" She didn't sound as if she would be pleased by whatever he said.

"I told the agents that you and Sweet would be staying with me."

"Oh you did?" Sash's tone was clipped. "And why would you say that?"

Brandon nodded toward the boy asleep in Sash's arms. "Because you're both physically and mentally exhausted. The doctor said that Sweet seemed fine physically, but psychologically he's been traumatized."

"I know what he said. And?"

"He doesn't need the additional trauma of having to wade through crowds of reporters for the next couple of weeks. He needs to rest, and so do you. That won't happen if you go back to your place. I have plenty of room for both of you here. This is a gated area. There's a security patrol and both of you will be protected from prying eyes if you stay here." Brandon tried not to appear too anxious about her decision.

Sash considered what he was saying. It did sound reasonable but she was reluctant to agree with Brandon in any way. "You never trusted me, Brandon. You all but called me a deceitful liar to my face since the day we met. I doubt if you trust anybody, so why would you want me to stay under your roof?"

Brandon could hardly believe that she was still holding his initial distrust of her against him. "Well you're right, Sash. I don't trust anybody and you can blame me all you want. There's nothing I can do about that. But I did what I felt was necessary and I thank God that things worked out and that Sweet is safe. Blame me all you want for what you perceive as my past transgressions, but right now, you and Sweet need time to heal and I want to offer the two of you the comfort and security that you need to help with that healing. I have the means and I have the opportunity to make the offer and with no strings attached, whether you believe me or not. If you don't want to stay here for yourself, fine, but at least do it for Sweet. After all he's been through he deserves the luxury of comfort and security. Now you think about that and let me know." Stiffly, Brandon walked from the room closing the door firmly behind him

Sash never felt so small. Brandon was right. What in the world was wrong with her? Instead of gratitude she was harboring resentment against a man who had helped save her brother's life. She owed Brandon a debt she could never repay, and she owed him an apology.

Brandon sat in his office nursing a scotch and soda. He wasn't a drinking man, but Sash Adams could drive any man to drink. What did she want from him anyway? She had already cost him a small fortune now burnt to a crisp! What did she want next? Blood?

Slamming the glass down on the desktop Brandon got up from the desk, walked to the window and looked out into the darkness. Why was he letting Sash get under his skin? Hell, he hardly knew the woman. So what if they had been through a lot together, he still shouldn't let her upset him as much as she did.

Brandon moved back to the desk and fell heavily into his chair. Fingering the crystal glass still filled with scotch, he stared into the amber liquid and sighed in resignation. He knew what the problem was and why Sash got to him the way that she did. He wanted her, and he wanted her to want him. And of course there was Sweet. He was quite a kid.

Remembering the crash site Brandon recalled his feelings of overwhelming fear and helplessness when Sash slipped into unconsciousness. He had been frantic when he gathered Sash in his arms to go get help for her, but his efforts were temporarily interrupted by a police officer exiting the darkened weeds. The officer was carrying a small bundle in his arms, a whimpering child, bruised and dirty but unharmed. It was Sweet. As they drew near, the child became aware of what was happening around him and he glanced down at Brandon. At that moment Brandon had nearly reeled as he recognized the eyes that met his own. He saw the resemblance immediately. The moment was electric, one he would never forget. The photo of Sweet that Brandon had harbored in his pocket for the last two days had come to life.

Over the past few hours he hadn't had the opportunity to spend any time alone with the boy and he wanted badly to get to know him. Of course the way Sash seemed to still feel about him, getting that chance might not be easy.

Brandon was considering the best way to approach this dilemma when there was a knock on the door. Expecting John Nathan he was surprised when Sash entered the room. He watched her slowly approach him, hands behind her back. He hoped she wasn't hiding a weapon. She stood looking at him for a moment before speaking.

"I owe you an apology, Brandon, and I'm here to say I'm sorry."

Brandon looked bewildered at this surprising turn of events. "Oh, really?"

"Yes. You helped save my brother's life. I can never repay you, and I'm sorry for being so rude. Plus I'm sorry about slapping you earlier. It was my foolish move that almost cost Sweet his life, not anything you did. The slap was uncalled for. I hope that you'll accept my apology."

Brandon nodded, pleased by her words. "You do carry quite a wallop, but I accept your apology, Sash, and I'm glad that things worked out."

Sash hesitated before continuing, not as certain about her next words as she had been about the apology. "If the invitation still stands I would like to accept your offer to stay here for a while. You're right about it being better for Sweet and—"

The sound of rapid footsteps in the hallway interrupted Sash's train of thought. A second later John Nathan burst into Brandon's office. He looked harried as his eyes swept the room. His suit jacket was pulled aside to reveal the revolver in his holster.

"What is it, John?" Brandon could see the man's concern.

"Sorry, Brandon, but I wanted to make sure you and Ms. Adams were okay. I already checked on the boy. We found two intruders on the grounds. Reporters."

Brandon frowned. "Reporters? How?"

"I wish I knew. Somehow they broke security. They got past the guard at the main gate, then it looks like they might have gotten on your property by way of the neighbor's place. My men caught them before they made it to the house. They're holding them now. We've called the local authorities."

"Good." John turned to leave but Brandon stopped him. "Tell me truthfully, John, will your guys be able to prevent breaches like this again?"

John was honest. "Truthfully, I don't think so. We can only do so much, and this thing is attracting a lot of press. You should see outside the gate. There are helicopters hovering about, too."

Brandon thought for a moment, remembering how aggressive he had been as a young reporter after a big story, and knowing how aggressive he encouraged his own reporters to be. How ironic that *he* should be the big story. Well he could handle it, but it wasn't fair that Sash and Sweet should have to. He turned to Sash. "You heard, John. It seems that my initial offer will have to be rescinded. I won't be able to protect the two of you here, but I've got another offer. I have a place where I can assure you that neither of you will be bothered until you're ready to leave. I'd like to extend the same invitation for you to stay there."

Sash shrugged. She was not anxious for her life or for Sweet's life to be invaded by hordes of media. "Fine, as long as Sweet is protected. Where are we going?"

Brandon grinned, hoping that she would be pleased by his answer. "Hawaii." The look of surprise followed by the grin on Sash's face told him that she was indeed pleased.

CHAPTER 14

"This is like being in heaven, isn't it Sash?" Sweet was beaming. His dark brown eyes were shining with excitement. Sash had never seen him so happy, even before the kidnapping. She fought back tears of joy.

"It sure is, honey," she replied, returning his smile. The child's description of their surroundings couldn't have been more appropriate.

They had arrived on Brandon's Hawaiian estate, Pineapple Hill, three weeks ago, the day after the breach of security at his home in Monterey. She and Sweet had slept most of the way as they were transported to the estate on Brandon's private plane. When they arrived at Pineapple Hill early the next morning, both she and Sweet were excited. The estate was located on a small, private island off Hawaii, or the Big Island, the largest of the state's eight major islands and the state's namesake. Pineapple Hill could only be reached by boat. On their arrival, neither Sash nor Sweet had any doubt that they had arrived in paradise.

Exotic trees, flowers and plants surrounded them as they walked the short distance from the ocean to the estate, which consisted of four one-story structures. Each was simplistic in its exterior design, but their breathtaking interiors paid homage to the nature around them. The main house contained Brandon's living quarters, including a master bedroom suite, an extra bedroom, and a state of the art kitchen. Every room in the house looked out onto the ocean beyond and the living room with its soaring 40 foot, wood beam ceiling was spectacular. The cathedral ceiling culminated in a skylight that allowed sunlight to flood the room's interior. Two guest pavilions flanked each side of the main house and were joined to it by flower lined walkways. Each of the three houses had pathways that led to a pool pavilion, topped by a thatched roof and supported by four wooden beams. Several garden showers with trellis ceilings were located within proximity of each of the buildings. The entire setting was picture perfect, very much like paradise.

On their arrival at Pineapple Hill, Sash and Sweet were settled in one of the guesthouses. They wasted little time in learning to enjoy their lavish surroundings. During the weeks that followed, Sash noticed a dramatic change in Sweet.

Since the death of their parents, when he was three, Sweet had often been a solemn little boy. Sash had made every effort to make sure that he knew that he was loved and cared about, but still she sensed that there was a void in his life that she couldn't seem to fill. Yet, in these past few weeks a different child was beginning to emerge—a child filled with new life.

As Sash wrapped Sweet in a thick oversized towel and wiped the pool water from his body, she noted how his nutmeg skin glowed. The Hawaiian sun had darkened him and the scrumptious meals that they had been treated to helped fill in his slender frame. The little boy before her was not only happier but also healthier. The anxieties she had feared would haunt him as the result of his abduction and fiery rescue appeared to be minimal and she had only one person to thank for all of this.

Shifting her eyes from her brother to the man emerging from the swimming pool, Sash felt her heartbeat quicken. The sight of Brandon Plaine in a pair of skimpy swim trunks should be against the law. The man was six foot three of muscular temptation; there was no doubt about it. She had avoided that temptation as steadily as she could during their time on the island. She didn't want to confuse her growing feelings for Brandon with the gratitude that she felt. She owed him so much. Not only had he helped save Sweet, but she also owed him for her brother's physical and mental well being. Lusting after the man was something she didn't need nor did he. Despite their initial conflicts, she and Brandon had developed a camaraderie during their time together in paradise that she would not have believed possible. Each chose to ignore the increasing sexual tension between them. Instead, they concentrated on their growing friendship.

During the day, after Brandon had put in a couple of hours of work via conference calls, fax and e-mail, he would join Sash and Sweet and the rest of his time would be theirs. The three of them would go fishing, boating, hiking, swimming in the ocean, each day exploring the island in some way. Brandon would spend endless hours talking to and playing with Sweet and after he was put to bed the evenings belonged to Sash and him. They would lounge in the stunning living room of the main house, sipping on tasty fruit drinks and talking for hours about everything under the sun, learning more about each other every day. They discovered that they had a lot in common, including having both lived in Africa as students. They entertained each other with endless stories about their various adventures. As the days turned into weeks, their friendship grew and their conversations began to turn more personal.

Brandon told her about his father, Harold Plaine. It was he who had founded the small, community newspaper, *The Caller*, that had eventually launched the Plaine Deal Media empire. Brandon's father had raised him alone after his mother abandoned them. Brandon had been five years old when his mother left, the same age as Sweet.

As Sash listened attentively to Brandon talk about his father, his adoration of the man was evident. He could hardly mask the pain that he still felt as he related to her how his father had died of a heart attack. Harold Plaine had been fifty-two years old. She could understand his pain.

"I was twelve years old when my father died," she recalled. "And I was heartbroken. When James Curry married my mother and became my stepfather I gave him holy hell."

"The poor man." Brandon quipped in empathy having been at the receiving end of Sash's displeasure.

Sash swatted at him, feigning insult at his teasing before continuing. "But James was so gentle and patient with me that it wasn't hard for him to win me over. He was a good man and I loved him very much. He was truly my second father. "

"Why didn't you get to know your stepsister, Shirley?" Brandon asked with cautious curiosity.

"Well, we were both adults. I was out of the house and on my own the one and only time we met, so we never got the opportunity to get to know each other well, " Sash replied, as she thought about the tall, willowy beauty that James had introduced to her as his daughter. His pride in the exquisite beauty had been obvious, but his daughter's contempt for James was equally as obvious. "Shirley and James had been estranged since he and her mother divorced. From what I could gather, Shirley's mother was bitter and turned her daughter against her ex-husband. James wanted to get close, but Shirley wouldn't let him. She was a grown woman, her mother was dead and she didn't have anyone else by the time she came back into James' life, and that was only briefly. It was sad, because James was a wonderful man." Sash sighed. "Shirley was a model and fairly successful at it, too, I was told. She was a beautiful woman. She seemed to have everything, but for some reason she wasn't happy. It was a shame."

In the reflective silence that followed that conversation, Brandon surprised Sash with a revelation of his own. "I had a brother," he said quietly.

The words were said with such sadness that Sash felt compelled to reach out and touch Brandon's hand. "You said *had.* What happened to him?"

Brandon closed his hand over her hand and rubbed his thumb gently over the palm. He seemed lost in thought before he answered her question. "He died."

"Oh, I'm sorry. Were you close?"

"We were twins, fraternal twins, but we weren't close. When she left, our mother took my brother with her and I didn't see him again until after she died. By then we were eighteen years old."

The picture of an older man with laughing eyes and a brooding young man that looked like Brandon flashed through Sash's memory. *That's not me.* That's what he had said when she inquired about the picture on his desk.

"Your parents separated twins?" She didn't try to conceal her disapproval. "So did you get to know him at least?" From Brandon's reaction talking about his brother didn't appear to be easy.

He gave a bitter laugh, "No, not as well as I thought."

Abruptly, Brandon changed the subject and avoided talking about personal subjects after that conversation. But, he did make sure that Sash was kept abreast of the developments surrounding Sweet's kidnapping.

All three people involved in the kidnapping had been identified. The man who had died in the car was named Louis Carlton, an ex-con with a criminal record that reached back to his teenage years. He had been out of San Quentin less than a year. The man who Sash had attacked was named Willie Dean. He had been in San Quentin with Carlton and had been released at the same time. Authorities had discovered Willie Dean's body in a shallow grave in the Santa Cruz mountains. He hadn't died from the injuries Sash had inflicted. He had died from a bullet wound from Carlton's gun.

Monee Sherman was the name of the woman who Sweet called "the lady." From all accounts she was a quiet, religious woman who worked as a school nurse. She had formerly lived in Richmond, California and was reportedly a frequent visitor to San Quentin to visit Carlton. She had started writing him as part of a church project to reach out spiritually to inmates. The authorities theorized that Monee was the catalyst for the kidnapping plot. Personnel records at Plaine Deal Media revealed that Monee had worked as a receptionist in one of the company's television stations while attending nursing school. Further details were unknown, and no one was alive to provide them but Monee who was still in a coma.

As the weeks passed, the interest and excitement about the kidnapping and the subsequent rescue was gradually subsiding. The headlines had turned to other concerns. Sash knew that soon she and Sweet would be returning home. Whether their lives would ever be normal again remained to be seen, but she was sure that returning wouldn't be easy, especially when they had to leave Brandon. From the day they set foot on the isolated island the man and the boy had been inseparable.

Sweet adored Brandon and it seemed that the feeling was reciprocated. Over the past few weeks Sweet's entire personality had changed. He balked at being called by the nickname that his parents had given him when he was a baby. Brandon called him "T" which was short for Trent. Sweet insisted that his old nickname was for babies. He talked insistently about what a big boy he was and how when he grew up he was going to be just as tall, just as strong, and just as brave as Brandon. Sash's fondest wish had been that her brother have a strong male role model. He had found one, and what a *male* he had picked as a model.

Sash turned her attention to the man in question as she watched his tall, muscular frame walk toward them. When he made his appearance at the swimming pool earlier, she hadn't known which part of his anatomy to lust after first. She had allowed herself the luxury of giving him a long, slow perusal of every inch of his masculine frame, from his broad shoulders marked by a cute little birthmark, down his chest sprinkled lightly with hair, to his lean, tight abdomen, which defined the term six pack. Somehow she had managed to keep her eyes from straying lower and lingering; but presently, as he walked toward them wiping the water from that delicious body, Sash found it difficult to keep her eyes above his waist.

While Sash's attention was riveted on Brandon, Sweet broke free from her and ran to him. Bending, he swept the child into the air, holding him high. Sweet's delighted squeals filled the air.

"I'm going to get you wet again," Brandon warned him as he shifted the boy in his arms. Sweet's arms and legs encircled Brandon's wet body.

"I don't care," Sweet responded, relaxing contentedly in the arms of his hero. He snuggled deeper into Brandon's body and gave him a quick kiss on the neck before laying his head on Brandon's shoulder. Brandon blinked rapidly and took a shaky breath.

Sash watched the interaction between the man and boy with a sense of satisfaction. It continued to amaze her how vulnerable this self-made media mogul appeared to be in the presence of this small child. She admired that about him. It seemed that lately every feeling she had toward Brandon was positive. That could make leaving him as hard on her as it would be on Sweet.

Having reached Sash in the dining area of the pool pavilion, Brandon sat down across from her in one of the rattan chairs, placing Sweet in his lap. If someone had told him a year ago that he could be totally captivated by a child he would have declared that person insane; but he was captivated. He was charmed and delighted by this little boy. The child was so innocent, so open, and so honest. He was completely under Sweet's spell. Brandon smoothed his hand gently over the boy's damp hair as the small, warm body rested against his own. The truth was that Trent Curry's spell wasn't the only spell under which he had fallen. The boy's sister was quite a spell weaver herself.

Brandon turned his attention to the woman sitting across the table from him. He had noticed Sash watching him when he emerged from the pool, and inwardly smiled at the thought that she might like what she saw. He knew that he was enjoying his view. The flowered, two piece swimsuit that she was wearing was torture on his body.

The woman had curves where curves were meant to be. How much was a healthy man suppose to take?

Luckily, Sash had taken mercy on his libido before he embarrassed himself and covered her torso with one of the oversized towels placed poolside for guests. He'd have to tell the housekeeper to purchase smaller towels in the future. Meanwhile, he could enjoy the abundance of chest the towel didn't conceal. Before they had spent time on this island, Brandon knew that he might want to be the man in Sash's life. Their time together on the island had only intensified his desire for her. However, time was running out for him. She would be leaving soon. He had to make his move, but he was worried that she might reject him based on past resentments. Hopefully, he was wrong.

Brandon glanced at Sash. She appeared preoccupied with her frothy pineapple drink. He wondered if she found him as big of a distraction as he found her to be. He knew she was interested in him. A little birdie had informed him of that fact. "Sash likes you," the birdie had chirped. "She likes you a lot. She told me so."

Armed with that information, Brandon's hopes had soared. He flashed a grateful smile at the birdie in his lap.

"Do you want a pineapple frosty, T?" There was no reply. Brandon looked down to find the boy asleep.

"Give him to me and I'll put him to bed," Sash said smiling fondly at her brother. She stood and reached for the boy.

"No." Brandon stood. "I'll do it. Just lead the way."

They worked together to strip Sweet of his wet bathing suit, dress him in fresh underwear and tuck him into bed. After closing the door behind them, they stepped into the living room where they stood face to face for a moment in awkward silence. They could feel the heat rising between them. Brandon's eyes were like lasers as he looked at Sash. Slowly he lowered his face to hers, but Sash took a step back.

She exhaled shakily. "Uh, I've got to take a shower."

Brandon's finger caressed her cheek. "We need to talk."

She wanted to lick his finger so badly that she could taste it. Instead she took another step back. "I thought we already solved all of the world's problems," she teased.

Brandon played along. "We have a few things that still need to be settled."

"Like what?" Sash grinned, feeling more at ease with this innocent flirtation. She was about to give a sigh of relief until Brandon threw her a curve.

"Like us."

"Us?" The grin on Sash's face vanished.

"That's what I said."

Sash swallowed and took two steps backward. "I hate to tell you this, Brandon, but there is no *us*."

"Maybe there should be." Brandon stepped forward. They were nearly chest to chest.

For a moment Sash felt disembodied. Things had been progressing so well, now all of a sudden there was an *us?*

She studied Brandon intently. His teasing eyes had turned serious. "What are you up to Brandon? What's this about?"

Brandon gave a sweeping gesture with his hands, encompassing Sweet, Sash and himself. "It's about the three of us and what we've come to mean to each other while we've been here on the island." He pointed to her and then to himself. "It's about you and me and what I hope we can mean to each other no matter where we are."

"Brandon, I'm grateful to you . . . "

"It's not your gratitude I want."

"But I don't like being obligated."

"Or that you be obligated to me."

"I've always paid my own way . . . "

"And you can continue to do so. This isn't about that either." Brandon moved closer to Sash, challenging her to retreat. She didn't.

"You know that Sweet has become quite fond of you," Sash started to babble.

"And I'm crazy about him, but that's not the topic of this discussion either."

"Brandon, I…"

"Brandon, I *what*? Brandon, I'm crazy about you?"

"I didn't say that."

"Then do say it, Sash, because I am crazy about you and I'm hoping that I'm not in this alone." Moving to the sofa Brandon sat down and tugged at her hand until she sat down beside him. He was determined that they were going to get to the bottom of their feelings for each other. "I'm through playing coy, Sash. Like I said, I'm crazy about you and I think that you're attracted to me, too. So tell me why you keep putting distance between us?"

Sash didn't answer. Instead, she sat contemplating his question.

"I'm waiting." Brandon informed her, leaning back and placing his ankle across his knee.

Sash started. He looked and sounded so much like Michael when he said that she had to take a cleansing breath to clear her head. All she had ever wanted from Brandon was trust and truth and he was presenting her with both. How could she offer him any less?

"You're right I am attracted to you, but Lord knows I don't want to be."

Brandon met her confession with mixed emotions. "Well I don't want to read that in a Hallmark card. Can you tell me what you mean by that?"

"I've had experience with men like you."

Brandon was amused by the observation. "What kind of man am I Sash?"

"Rich, powerful, arrogant, a man used to giving orders, not accepting compromise—a man who likes dependent women."

"Oh really?" He raised a brow.

"Yes. I've been involved with one rich and powerful man who tried to erode my self-confidence and disregarded my dreams and ambitions. I'm not about to let that happen again."

Brandon was taken aback. He assumed that she was talking about Michael and he didn't like the comparison. "Well, I'm my own person, Sash, so don't get me confused with someone else."

Sash rose from the sofa and looked down at him. "You may not be *that* man, Brandon, but there have been occasions in the past when you've shown me the same tendencies."

Brandon rose, not noticing the wet spots that each of their damp swimsuits had left on the colorful sofa. He was preoccupied with the anger he felt at the thought that Sash would compare him to Michael.

"I'll tell you what. It's obvious that we need to discuss this further. So why don't you go take your shower and meet me at the pool pavilion in, say, thirty minutes." Brandon exited the room stiffly, not waiting to hear whether she would meet him or not.

Sash continued to stand rooted after the door closed behind him. It appeared that the kisses she had shared with Brandon when they were in pursuit of Sweet's freedom had held promises that were soon to be claimed.

CHAPTER 15

Sash. He could hear the sound of her name reverberate in the waves that performed their ceremonial dance on shore. As Brandon stood watching the sea's ancient ritual his mind and body were filled with her. When had this impossible woman with her dreadlocked hair, her Zen-like philosophy and her eclectic style of life crept inside his heart? She was nothing like the woman he usually was attracted to. She wasn't interested in high fashion, or pop art or belonging to the "right" clubs. To Sash the word civic duty meant more than attending a charity ball. The other women he knew all seemed superficial next to her. Money and status weren't her constant pursuits. No, not Sash. Her career goal was to become an attorney that helped the poor. She actually believed that good could overcome evil. Sash was unique—tough, bold, independent and as opinionated as hell.

How in the world had he fallen so hard for this woman? They were oil and water. Yet, he knew the answer to his question. Sash was a dynamo, to say nothing of her intelligence, creativity and beauty. The woman was lethal to his well-being. He had never planned on giving his heart away again to any woman. He had made that mistake before, but Sash was under his skin like an itch that wouldn't go away. Each day she burrowed a little deeper. He was a mere heartbeat away from falling in love with her, and the thought of what that might mean to his psyche was scaring him to death.

While Brandon's heart still might be trying to resist Sash's intrusion, it had surrendered completely to Sweet. He acted like a lunatic trying to please the boy and relished every moment of the time spent with him. Never could Brandon have imagined that someone so small could so thoroughly control his emotions. He wanted that feeling to continue, but with the stance that Sash was taking about him he wasn't sure what would happen. Yet one thing seemed fairly certain, when John Nathan brought the news that he expected him to bring it could change everything.

Brandon gave a wistful sigh. Looking up, he could see the formation of storm clouds over the ocean rapidly moving toward the estate. A rising wind was causing ripples in the ocean's serenity. It occurred to him that the scene he was witnessing could be a preview of what was to come in his own life. Turning, he headed toward the house. There was just enough time to bathe, dress and meet Sash.

Spurred by the rain shower that caught him before he could reach the main house, Brandon stepped into the nearest garden shower. He welcomed the tranquility of the shower's interior. It was like stepping into a tropical jungle. Plants strategically placed in the structure's enclosure, rose to the aged wood lattice ceiling that opened to the sky. Other plants hung from hooks attached to the lattice. Two of the shower's four walls were covered with ivy. Another wall contained the shower and he couldn't wait to savor its welcoming spray.

Stepping into a pair of the disposable shower shoes placed in a neat row at the shower's entrance, Brandon slipped out of his swim trunks and stood to venture farther into the structure. A startled cry halted his steps. He looked up to see Sash standing before him completely nude.

She resembled a wood nymph standing there against the backdrop of forest greenery. Mist from the rain falling through the opened ceiling engulfed her frozen form. Her arms were crossed protectively across her breast. Her brown body was sleek, glistening with moisture. Brandon tried hard to keep his eyes focused on Sash's face, but was unsuccessful as he stood speechless, immobile. However, the rest of his body failed to cooperate with his immobility. His member hardened immediately.

"What are you doing here?" Sash's voice was a high pitched shriek. Still reeling from the shock of Brandon intruding on her impromptu rain shower her chest heaved from indignation and embarrassment. It was clear that his body was ready for more than bathing and the look in his eyes warned her that he was capable of fulfilling his body's desire.

Brandon's mouth was completely dry. He found it difficult to breathe. His lips moved but the words wouldn't come. For what seemed like forever he stood mesmerized, drinking in the sight of Sash's naked beauty. Finally he managed to croak. "Sorry." The voice sounded nothing like his own.

The silence that followed his apology was interrupted only by the sound of the rain. Thunder rumbled in the distance, lightening illuminated the darkened sky. Rain drops danced off their naked bodies as Brandon and Sash stood nude in the forest like setting—Adam and Eve in paradise, alone in the garden, and tempted.

Sash watched and waited. Her breathing becoming labored as the heat of desire spiraled through her. It was if she was possessed. Who was this wanton woman standing naked before this man as the rain turned to steam against her heated body? She should make a hasty retreat and run as far and as fast as her legs could take her. Yet, she stood there as still as stone, smothering under his gaze.

The pounding of Brandon's heart beat to the rhythm of the rain against his naked body. His brain implored his body to move but his body refused to listen. In a fog, he watched as Sash grabbed a towel from a brass hook, covered her nudity and floated silently toward him. Her eyes never left his. She passed him preparing to exit and her body heat singed him. Gingerly, he reached out and plucked the towel from her body.

As if in a trance Sash turned to face Brandon and with that single movement a mutual decision was made. Their eyes held. He drew her to him. Flesh met flesh as his lips took possession of her mouth and Brandon staked his claim.

Fissions of heat snaked without detour straight to Sash's core. Brandon pressed his firm erection against her and deepened the kiss. It became wild, fiery. Sash moaned her pleasure. Tearing his lips from hers, the tip of his tongue languidly encircled her nipple. It peaked. Lavishly, he suckled. Her moans of pleasure escalated, competing with splattering raindrops.

Brandon's nibble fingers snaked slowly down the length of her body and gripped her hips, drawing Sash closer and closer to him. He would allow nothing between them. His lips traveled up the slim column of Sash's throat and returned to her mouth where he inhaled her, breathed life into her, then took it back again. The sensations passing between them were invigorating, stimulating. Shaken, Brandon broke the kiss and took a ragged breath. He let his head fall limply in the cotton softness of Sash's wet hair. He reveled in the feel of her shapely, water soaked body against his own. This woman was an enchantress weaving a spell over him. What he was feeling for Sash was far more dangerous than lust. As he struggled to breathe and to regain hold of his erratic emotions, all of the pent up desire for the woman in his arms was expressed in the exhalation of one breathless word, "Sash."

Sash felt boneless as she lay against Brandon's broad chest listening to his rapid heartbeat. Her body trembled from his erotic assault. She sought to answer the need that she heard echoed in the whisper of her name. With confident fingers she lifted his face to hers and with lips of equal fire she lay her own claim and opened her heart to the possibilities. *Maybe it could work. Maybe they could make it. Maybe they could be good together.*

Sash's tongue glided smoothly to music composed by her body's creation while her hand took possession of Brandon's engorged shaft and created rhythms that made him dance to her command. It was Brandon's turn to moan. She deepened the kiss and increased the pressure. Brandon growled and backed Sash against the garden wall. She broke the kiss in an effort to exhale, but her effort was short-lived. With shaking hands Brandon removed Sash's deadly hand from his throbbing shaft and reigned kisses down the path of her heated body to the entrance to paradise. His hands played duets on the twin mounds of her hardened nipples while his tongue dabbled skillfully. The sound of his name, screamed in sweet completion, joined the roar of thunder rumbling across the sky. Sash's knees buckled. Strong arms were there to catch her as Brandon swept her up into his arms and carried her to the main house.

Once inside Brandon placed her on the bed. Abandoning her for even a second was excruciating but necessary. He locked the door, then hurried to the wicker dresser near the bed. Jerking the drawers open, Brandon tossed sheets, blankets and towels aside until he found the foil pouches that he had been seeking. Tearing one open, he covered his shaft before returning to her. Sash greeted him with eyes burning as bright as the desire in his own.

Their eyes held as he knelt above her. She reached up and nipped his nipple, then laved it lovingly with her tongue. Brandon swayed. "I can't take much more, Sash," he moaned.

She gave him a mysterious smile and proceeded to test his resolve. One renegade finger zigzagged slowly through the hair on his chest to rest once more on his hardened member. There an oval shaped fingernail drew skillful circles that brought groans of delight. Brandon shuttered and nearly lost it. Inhaling deeply, it took Herculean effort to maintain self-control. Opening glazed eyes, he brought the talented finger to his lips and placed a kiss on its tip. He planted a second kiss in the palm of Sash's hand. Then kneeing her legs apart he placed her hot little hand on his throbbing shaft once again. Together they guided his manhood into her inner sanctum.

Brandon felt Sash tense as he started to enter her body. "Talk to me, Sash," his voice implored as his eyes bored into her.

The entreaty reached Sash's muddled brain as she tried to make sense of what he was saying. *Talk?* She could hardly breath. "It's been a while," she managed to mumble.

Brandon understood. "Tell me how you feel." He moved slowly within her. "Are you all right?"

"Good," came her strangled reply.

Brandon increased the tempo making it better.

"So good." It was a declaration shouted to the stormy sky.

Sash arched her back and Brandon plunged deeper within her, their bodies moving in perfect union, having found their rhythm. Sash felt the fire of their union burning within her. Brandon rocked his hips and stiffened and she felt the power, his power, her power their power rising to the surface like a bubbling caldron of lava flowing from its volcanic source—hot, sizzling and ready to explode.

* * *

Brandon lay in a daze in the afterglow of having made love to Sash. His limbs were quaking from the intensity of their union. Before they made love he had wondered if Sash had bewitched him. Now, he had no doubt about it.

He was an experienced man, in control of every aspect of his life. Yet, looking down at Sash's sienna brown beauty he wondered how she could sleep so peacefully after she had sent his world spinning off its axis. Didn't she realize that she had stolen his heart? As he lay beside her, still hot and throbbing, he wasn't so sure that she didn't own his body as well.

A restless Sash stirred and Brandon drew her closer to him. He placed a kiss on one sculptured cheekbone. She threw a leg across his body and rubbed against him. Brandon's member rose in response. Need shot through him with the impact of a cannon. He ran a gentle finger down one soft cheek and with purpose, coaxed her awake with feathered kisses.

Slowly, Sash opened sparkling eyes as her rich, full lips bestowed on him a heart-stopping smile. It was replaced by a satisfied groan as Brandon turned his attention to her turgid breast. Sparked by his loving, Sash's nipples reawakened as her body welcomed him anew.

Brandon made love to her with everything he had to give, and Sash responded to him in return. It was at that moment that he made a solemn vow. He would do everything he could to make Sash Adams his.

CHAPTER 16

The enamored lovers wanted to languish in bed forever, sharing the wonder of their newfound relationship, but there was a small child in the house who had other ideas. By the time Sash left Brandon's bedroom, bathed away the vestiges of their lovemaking and dressed, Sweet had awakened and was looking for playmates. She and Brandon happily complied.

The three of them roamed the island on bicycles, stopping occasionally to explore uncharted territory. Later, at dinner Sweet chattered incessantly recounting the day's adventures, while the adults listened attentively with what appeared to be permanent smiles etched on their faces. They had experienced quite an adventurous day themselves, one that neither one of them could forget.

As the shadows of the day's end settled on the island, Brandon and Sweet ended it by playing a spirited game of checkers. The game was interrupted by a telephone call to Brandon. It was from John Nathan.

While Brandon was talking to John, Sash put an end to the checker game and coaxed a resistant Sweet to the guesthouse to ready him for bed. After completing his telephone call Brandon joined her and tucked Sweet in for the night. As he read him a bedtime story, enhanced with action, Sash studied Brandon. He was exuberant, animated. There seemed to be a quiet excitement radiating from him that she hadn't noticed before. Was it a result of what was developing between them? She wasn't certain how he defined the feelings he was experiencing, but she was certain of what she felt. It was love, and it had hit her hard and fast.

Who would have thought that she could ever have fallen for this man, with all of his complexities? But she had. She could feel his essence down to her toes. Making love with him had been the most sensuous experience that she had ever had. She had never been so wanton. She had given herself to Brandon completely, more than she had to anyone before. It had shaken her. It also frightened her. This feeling for Brandon was deep. It had sneaked up on her quickly, unexpectedly and it made her feel vulnerable. Earlier that morning she had awakened as a solo act. Was she now one half of a pair? That's how she felt, not half of a person, but part of a whole. It was a strange feeling, but she knew that what happened between the two of them had been more than a brief interlude.

After they left Sweet's room Brandon took her in his arms and placed a kiss on her lips. "Come on. Let's go talk."

They strolled back to the main house hand in hand and sat cuddled together on the sofa in his spectacular living room. Brandon wasted no time getting to what he wanted to discuss.

"I'm not a man who expresses his feelings easily, Sash, I think you know that by now. But I want to let you know that what I feel for you runs deep." His voice was husky.

His look was intent. "I don't do casual sex, and I can tell you that making love with you earlier meant a lot to me and I hope that it meant the same to you, too."

Sash looked into Brandon's eyes and saw the truth in his words. What he was saying and doing was significant for him. He was opening himself up to her and she could do no less. "It does, Brandon. Believe me it does. I care about you very much, but…"

Brandon stiffened, "But what?"

Reluctantly, Sash peeled herself from Brandon's arms to face him. She wanted no misunderstanding about what she was about to say.

"But you must understand that whatever decisions that I make in my life I always have to think about what's best for Sweet."

Brandon gave an audible sigh of relief. The turn in the conversation was perfect. "I have no doubt about that, Sash. I've been a living witness to how much you love your brother and I've make no secret that I'm crazy about him, too. I've come to love him as much as I've come to—" Brandon caught himself, surprised at what he was about to say. He cleared his throat. "Believe me, when it comes to Sweet and his welfare you'll never have to worry as far as I'm concerned. As a matter of fact, it's Sweet I need to talk to you about."

"Oh? What about him?"

A kaleidoscope of emotions danced across Brandon's face. He sat back and took a deep breath before speaking. "Well, I think that if you and I got together it would be very good for him."

Surprised, Sash cocked her head and looked at Brandon. "Oh, really?"

"Yes, really." Brandon's eyes glowed with excitement. "Let me show you something." He withdrew a leather wallet from the pocket of his khaki shorts and removed a small photograph. He handed it to Sash.

At first glance it appeared to be a photograph of Sweet grinning at the camera. There was no threat to the life of this child. His eyes were sparkling with mischief. His face was alive with hope. Sash examined the photo closer. The child did look a lot like her brother, but the boy in the photo wasn't Sweet. An unsettling feeling formed in the pit of Sash's stomach. Her eyes slowly rose to meet Brandon's eyes.

"Who is this?"

"My brother, Brice." Brandon paused and looked at Sash steadily. " My father's nickname for him was Buddy."

Sash's stomach dropped. She closed her eyes to regroup.

"Are you all right?" Brandon sounded anxious.

Opening her eyes, Sash nodded. The final pieces of the puzzle were beginning to fit. "Go on." Her voice was hollow.

"The kidnappers knew so much, about Brice, his nickname, even about the butterfly tattoo."

"Butterfly? I remember that. But what's this about a tattoo?"

"Our birthmarks. Brice and I both were born with birthmarks on our shoulders. His was shaped like a butterfly and Dad used to call it his butterfly tattoo." Brandon swallowed the emotions that renewed themselves at the memory.

"So you recognized those things from what I told you and from my notebook. That's why you changed your mind about helping me." Her mind raced. "You asked me about his adoption. Do you think that Sweet is related to you?"

"I think he's my nephew."

"How can that be? Sweet's biological father's last name was..."

"Raymond."

"Yes. I told you that before."

"I remember, but you can see the resemblance. As soon as I saw the picture you gave me, I thought about this one." He took the photograph from Sash's hand and studied it. "It was like looking at Brice all over again. He and I were five years old when we took these school pictures. Our mother left with him the next day." There was a catch in Brandon's voice.

Carefully, he tucked the picture back in his wallet. The action gave him time to regain a semblance of control. Running his hand over his face, he tried to wipe away the painful memories; but he had tried most of his life and failed. "When she left Dad and took one of his sons it nearly killed my father. I don't think that he ever really recovered from her deception. He spent most of his life and most of his money looking for her and Brice. I believe that if Dad had found her he would have begged her to come back to him. He loved her that much. He never said one negative word to me about her, even though she left him for another man. Later we discovered that's why he couldn't find her. She had changed her last name and Brice's to her lover's last name. She started calling Brice by his middle name." Brandon paused, his eyes boring into Sash's eyes.

"Her lover's last name was Raymond. My brother's name was changed from Brice Leon Plaine to Leon Raymond."

"My stepsister's husband." The air sucked from Sash's lungs. The full scope of the unfolding scenario sent a chill through her body. "Did you know for certain that Sweet might be your nephew when I told you about Shirley?"

"I knew that the name fit, but I still wasn't certain. As far as I knew Brice and Shirley didn't have any children." Brandon took Sash's hand in his. It was cold. "Actually, I knew very little about my brother. You see he was out of my life for thirteen years. Then one day he popped up at my father's office and announced that our mother was dead. He told us that after our mother died his stepfather, who he thought was his biological father, told him about Dad and me. It seems that our mother and her lover hadn't done as well as they thought they would together. This Raymond character sought comfort in a bottle and our mother kept him company. They both were drunks."

Brandon dropped Sash's hands, stood and jammed his hands in his pocket. He wandered the room as he spoke. The anger and bitterness was as fresh as if it were yesterday.

"I like to think that she took to the bottle because of a guilty conscience. I often wonder if she knew what she'd done to me and Dad. Or did she even care." He stopped pacing momentarily to stare into the past before shaking himself back to the present.

"Anyway, she died from cirrhosis of the liver. A few months later, Raymond died from exposure. He fell asleep in a drunken stupor in some alley. The temperature was below zero—a fitting end I guess."

Brandon paused again to assess his feelings. The tragic deaths of the two people who had nearly destroyed his father hadn't left him feeling as satisfied as he thought. He had spent most of his life wondering why his mother didn't love him. Why had she taken Brice and not him? Until he found out about her untimely death he thought that he hated her for having made such a choice. The truth was that he loved her and yearned for her return. With her death he would never know the answer to the one question that had haunted him most of his life. *Why?*

As Sash watched Brandon struggle with his emotional demons so much about this complicated man became crystal clear. The pain of lost and abandonment was as acute for him now as it had been when he was a child. His incessant drive for wealth, power, and control had been motivated by the need to prove that he was worthy—worthy of being cared for, worthy of being loved and worthy of not being abandoned.

Rising, Sash put her own feelings of turmoil aside and went to Brandon. She wrapped her arms around him, resting her cheek on his broad back. She knew without a word from him that he needed her touch. He responded, wrapping his arms around her arms in silent gratitude. She could feel him relax against the weight of her body. Gently, she prodded him to continue his story.

"So Brice showed up when you two were eighteen. Did the two of you become friends at all?"

Brandon turned to face her. He gave a heavy sigh. "Unfortunately no. Life had been hard for Brice, moving from pillar to post, transferring from one school to another. He had never acquired friends or had any stability, and it seemed that this Raymond fellow was physically abusive. He told us that he hated him. Yet, Brice also resented my father. He blamed him for not rescuing him. He told Dad that he should have looked for him harder. Dad tried so hard to have a relationship with him. He was so happy to have Brice back in his life. You know that picture that I have of him and Brice in my office?"

"Yes. "

"I keep it because it's the happiest memory I have of my father with Brice. Dad tried everything to make up for the past, but nothing worked. Brice was hostile and bitter. He took advantage of Dad's kindness in every way he could. And he resented me even more. He told me once that I had everything and he had grown up with nothing." Brandon gave a shaky sigh. "But he was only half right. I did have Dad, thank God for that, but Brice had our mother."

Brandon went on to tell Sash about the clashes between he and Brice. Like his mother and stepfather, Brice struggled with alcohol and drugs. Eventually, he stormed out of their father's house after a fight with Brandon and wasn't seen or heard from for over a decade.

"He reappeared out of nowhere with no warning," Brandon told her as they returned to the sofa and back into each other's arms. "He swore that he was sober and I believed him. Dad was gone by then and Plaine Deal Media had taken off like a rocket. I offered him a job."

"Did the other employees know that he was your brother?"

"Actually, they didn't get a chance to meet him. He never showed up for work."

Sash wasn't surprised. She had never met Leon Raymond, but she had heard about him through her stepfather. According to him, Leon, or Brice, as Brandon called him, was an irresponsible hustler who died from a drug overdose, leaving his wife Shirley destitute and pregnant. After Shirley's death her parents had adopted Sweet, who was a toddler by then, and he became the light of their lives. She filled in the blanks for Brandon. He gave her a sad smile after she finished.

"I knew that Brice had died of an overdose but I didn't know what had happened to Shirley."

"She died from an overdose, too," Sash informed him. "A deliberate overdose of sleeping pills." There was a pregnant pause before she continued. "Do you know how Shirley and Brice met? Nobody in the family knew much about him."

Once again, Brandon rose, unable to sit at the avalanche of memories. He walked to the wall of windows and looked out. "Shirley and Brice met at a party in San Francisco. I guess it was love at first sight." Brandon snorted contemptuously. "Who knows. Anyway, a couple of weeks after they met, Brice disappeared for the last time, and took Shirley with him. That was six years ago and I never saw him again, nor did I bother to look for him. I was through. I'd have enough. It was only by accident that I found out he had died. I didn't know what had happened to Shirley and I knew absolutely nothing about Sweet."

Sash joined Brandon at the window, finding some sense of solace in looking out into the darkness beyond. This time she didn't touch him, but stood beside him. "So, now you do know about him. Have you told the authorities what you've told me?"

"No, although I know I should have. I didn't want any leaks to the press until I'm certain that Sweet is my nephew."

"It certainly sounds like he is and it sure explains why you were targeted for the ransom. But how would Carlton and his crew know about Brice? Monee worked for Plaine Deal Media in another state and from what you've told me it wasn't general knowledge that you even had a brother."

"I don't know, but tomorrow one mystery will be solved. John is coming to the island and he'll be bringing proof as to whether Sweet is Brice's son." Brandon turned to Sash. "I didn't tell you this earlier, but I had my doctor take a sample of Sweet's saliva, for a DNA test. Tomorrow I'll know for sure if Sweet is my nephew."

Hugging herself, Sash closed her eyes. "It doesn't take a brain surgeon to figure out the obvious. That is unless you have doubts about Shirley's loyalty to Brice."

Brandon didn't answer, but she could tell by his body language that he thought Shirley might be suspect. She decided not to pursue that issue. There had been enough revelations for one day.

Sash felt numb. She wasn't sure what to think or what lay ahead for the three of them.

Gently, Brandon gripped Sash's arms. "I'm sorry I didn't tell you all of this sooner, but things between the two of us were rocky enough when we came to Pineapple Hill. I was afraid that knowing that Sweet might be a part of me might make things even worse. But now that you know, now that we have feelings for each other—" He planted a kiss on her forehead and gathered her to him. "I don't want this to change things between us for the worse. Whatever happens I hope it will only make things better."

Sash slipped out of Brandon's embrace. "You should have shared this with me earlier. I realize you have a problem with trust, but..."

"Sash—" Brandon made a move toward her. She moved away.

"What you've told me is major, Brandon. Who knows what's going to become of the three of us as the result of this. So I say let's see what tomorrow brings and we'll play it by ear from there."

Brandon reviewed the suggestion in his mind. As long as she wasn't shutting the door between them they still had a chance. "That sounds fair."

Sash hugged herself, finding solace in the action. Maybe things would work out. Yet the feeling of anxiety stirring deep in the pit of her stomach would not go away.

* * *

John Nathan arrived the next day with more news than they expected. There would be no trail, no tabloid headlines. Everyone involved in the kidnapping of Sweet and Sash was dead. Monee Sherman had passed away without regaining consciousness. Although Sash held no great love for the woman because of her involvement with the kidnapping, Monee had saved Sweet's life. For that fact, if nothing else, Sash was sorry to hear about her demise.

Good detective work by the FBI had uncovered the sequence of events that led up to the kidnap plot. However, the authorities had discovered additional information about Monee Sherman that was even more revealing.

"They will probably be contacting the both of you, Brandon, so that they can talk with you further," said John.

"And why would they want to do that?" Sash asked, not looking forward to the idea of having to deal with the FBI again.

"Because they discovered that Monee worked as a nurse in the hospital in New Jersey where Sweet was born."

Brandon and Sash exchanged glances. It took little imagination to assume that Monee must have befriended Sweet's biological mother and that secrets had been revealed—secrets that in the future would be worth a king's ransom.

"They know that Sweet was adopted and they're looking into the files now to trace his biological parents. If there turns out to be a connection between you and the boy at all, Brandon, I'd advise you to let the authorities know." John implored.

Brandon remained silent. He would buy all of the time he could for the child before the media circus began.

John continued. "Anyway, the authorities haven't found anyone else involved in the case. So, it's over."

Both Sash and Brandon breathed sighs of relief.

"Now, about that other matter." John withdrew several envelopes from the briefcase he was carrying. He took a small bundle of envelopes held together by rubber bands and handed them to Sash. "Brandon asked me to drop by your house for your mail. Your landlady, Mrs. Rosemont, sent these to you."

Sash took the mail from John and thanked both men, bestowing a special smile on Brandon for his thoughtfulness. John then handed Brandon the single envelope for which he had been waiting. It contained the DNA information. With that, John acknowledged Brandon's expression of gratitude and excused himself from the room.

It was so quiet in the room that the ocean waves could be heard in the distance lapping against the shore. Sash sat waiting with baited breath as Brandon examined the white envelope. Growing impatient she was unable to take the suspense any longer.

"Please, just go ahead and open it."

With a shaky sigh, Brandon complied. Silently, he read

the contents while Sash watched him closely. Once again Brandon's lengthy examination of the contents caused Sash to intervene.

"What does it say?"

This time Brandon made her wait. The paper he was holding shook in his hands as he read the results. Briefly, he closed his eyes, opened them again and reread the words on the paper.

As she watched and waited Sash was beside herself. Her voice trembled with tension. "Brandon? Is there a DNA match or not?"

She started to rise, go to him and read the results for herself, but his words froze her in place.

"There's a match." Brandon crumbled the letter in his fist and raised watery eyes to Sash.

She fell back in her seat. Shock waves rippled through her body. She watched as Brandon turned and left the room. She didn't try to stop him.

Sash thought that she would be prepared to hear those three words, but she discovered that she was not. Her Sweet, her precious little boy, the most important person in her world no longer belonged to her alone. Now he had become apart of Brandon's world. What did it mean? Where would it lead? What would the future bring?

CHAPTER 17

Sash slowly opened her eyes, unsure of what had awakened her until she heard Brandon's footsteps move stealthily across the room and straight to her bedside. She lay still as death, nude beneath her bathrobe and resting on top of the bedspread. The bed sagged from Brandon's weight as he joined her, wrapping his body around her, engulfing her in his warmth. His fingers entwined with her fingers and she noticed that his fingers were cold, just as hers had been earlier. She squeezed them to let him know that she was awake and waiting.

Sash had left the main house when Brandon had not reappeared. His reaction to his unexpected fortune disturbed her. This man had gained the Holy Grail—a child she would have died for was now his to love. Brandon should be floating on air. Yet, she could feel his sadness as he lay beside her.

Sash turned in Brandon's arms to face him. Moonlight filtering into the room from the skylight silhouetted his profile.

"Are you afraid, Brandon? Does the responsibility of being more to Sweet frighten you?"

Her words filled the void in the darkness surrounding them, offering light that would allow them both to find their way. Yet, Brandon remained silent. Instead, slowly, deliberately he traced her full lips with his finger, committing them to memory; then, he leaned down and kissed her, gently at first, gradually growing in intensity. His tongue prodded the depths of her mouth's interior, demanding compliance. Sash leaned into him her body blossoming. Their need was mutual, radiated in the heat emanating from their bodies. Brandon's kiss grew deeper, harsher almost brutal in its ever increasing ardor.

Breaking the kiss, his persistent hands parted her garment. His eager tongue feasted on distended nipples with such fervor that Sash pleaded for release.

"Brandon, please!" she panted, fighting for every breath. Her hands roamed his body relentlessly, pushing, pulling, kneading and needing as his touch drove her into the abyss of madness.

"Sash." This is the woman he wanted. "Sash." This is the woman he needed. Sash!" This was the one who could assuage all of his wants and needs. His tongue basked in the swirl of her navel; one long-boned finger prepared the way for entry. She bucked upward and moaned in completion. Brandon left her no time for recovery. With one slight movement he straddled her, crushing her beneath him. The depths of his fervent lovemaking bordered on the brink of being out of control.

Sash's mind reeled as Brandon hungrily devoured her, gluttonous in his primal need. Once again the firestorm raged. Sash reached for him, ready to satisfy and be satisfied. But, as suddenly as it began the firestorm ended. Brandon rolled from her body and onto his back. Covering his eyes with one arm his breathless gasps echoed in the darkness.

Dazed and confused, Sash turned and reached out to him, her hand accidentally grazing the engorged evidence of Brandon's physical need. Yet, it was the source of his emotional need of which she was unsure. When she had gained some semblance of control her request was simple.

"Talk to me, Brandon."

The irony of her words didn't escape him. He had said those very words to her while they lay together mere hours ago, but the circumstances were so very different then. With much effort, Brandon moved from the bed, turned on the lamp and sat in a chair next to the bed. To stay in the bed with Sash was much too tempting. Still he reached for her, despite his effort to put a distance between them. He wanted her close to him. He *needed* her close to him. He wanted and needed her, period.

"Come here."

Righting her robe, Sash went to him. Brandon settled her on his lap and she waited.

"I'm sorry, Sash. I couldn't just use you like that. I care for you too much."

Sash reached up and caressed his cheek, warmed by his words. "Thank you for that."

Brandon kissed the palm of her hand, then reached into his pocket and withdrew the crumbled letter that he had jammed into his pocket earlier. It had been smoothed and neatly folded. He handed it to Sash. She glanced at the letter then back at Brandon.

Pushing herself off of his lap, Sash sat down on the side of the bed. Her body felt like lead. Something was wrong.

Her hand trembled as she started to open the letter. Once again her eyes went to Brandon's eyes. It was at that moment that the truth was silently exchanged.

He didn't have to tell her what was in the letter. She knew. Over the past few weeks there had been clues. *Why didn't you tell me that Sweet was adopted?* Innuendoes. *"Shirley and Brice met at a party in San Francisco. I guess that it was love at first sight."* Reality checks. *"There's a match."* No. She didn't have to read the letter. She knew what it said.

"Sweet is your son."

"Yes, he is." There were tears in his voice.

Sash breathed around the lump that worked its way to her throat. "Did you ever suspect that he was yours?"

"It never crossed my mind. I wanted the DNA match to prove that I was Sweet's uncle, not his father."

Her eyes fell to the paper in her hands. "There's no doubt about it?"

"99.8% according to the DNA."

Sash's eyes returned to Brandon. "It was you who introduced them at that party, wasn't it."

"Ironic, isn't it."

"Did you love her?" She could only hope that he would tell her the truth. She couldn't live with another deception.

Brandon looked her in the eye. "Yes I did, but obviously I didn't love her enough. She wanted to get married, but I wasn't ready for the ring and roses. We fought and she told me then that I would pay. I didn't know how high the price would be."

Without reading it, Sash handed the letter back to Brandon. "I wonder if your brother knew that Sweet wasn't his?"

"I wonder, too." Brandon studied the folded paper in his hand. "But *she* knew, and that's what hurts so bad."

As Sash watched Brandon return the letter to his pocket her heart broke for him. Abandoned by his mother, betrayed by his brother and by the woman that he loved, how could trusting anyone be anything but a challenge for him? The twist and turn of both their lives, as well as Sweet's, were all being controlled by choices made by others in the past.

"It's so unfair," Sash said more to herself than to Brandon. "But..." She squared her shoulders and addressed him directly. "Like I've said before, I have to think about Sweet and what's best for him."

Brandon agreed. It was Sweet who had been on his mind when he entered the guesthouse earlier, still stunned by the revelation that Trent Curry was his son. The shock of the DNA report had resulted in a myriad of emotions that ran the gamut from confusion to rage. He had roamed the estate for hours trying to sort it all out.

Finally, compelled by the need to reconcile the surreal with reality, Brandon had crept into Sweet's room and watched him as he was sleeping. His heart felt as if would burst. This was *his* flesh. *His* blood flowed through this child's veins. This beautiful child had become his own.

He studied the boy's features. There was a slight resemblance to him. Sweet had his chin and Sweet did have his eyes. Brandon jerked back, startled when those dark brown eyes suddenly opened and looked up at him. The boy flashed him a sleepy grin.

"Mr. B., I gotta use the bathroom." He said it as nonchalantly as if his waking up and finding Brandon in his room was the most natural thing in the world. Sweet reached out to him and Brandon picked him up and held his little body close to his own. He hugged him tightly and showered him with kisses, so many kisses that Sweet pushed away from him.

"Mr. B, you kissing me like a girl," Sweet protested swiping at the kisses on his cheeks with both hands.

The gesture was a special one between Sweet and his sister. Now Brandon was included, too. He had barely been able to hold back the tears. After Sweet had used the bathroom, at the boy's insistence Brandon read him a bedtime story. The child was asleep within five minutes and he had kissed Sweet again, then sat by his son's bed for an hour simply watching him breathe. As he did so all of the hurt and anger at his having been denied his child had resurfaced and he had gone to Sash's room to seek solace in her arms. But he found that his feelings for Sash wouldn't allow him to use her as simply a vessel for the release of his pain. His feelings for her ran so much deeper than that, much deeper than he had realized.

Now as Brandon sat across from Sash his anger gradually dissipated. He couldn't change the past, but he could make plans for the present and for the future. Everything he wanted and needed was within the walls of this house. He had been handed the opportunity to love again, not only to love a woman, but also to love a child. His own child.

He was a father! Fatherhood was the one thing in his life that had always been constant for him, the one thing that he could always trust. Once he got through the pain of the past, the future looked bright. He would make a good father. A great father! The thought of it excited him.

"Everything will work out fine, Brandon. You'll see. We'll

get through this." Sash reached out and covered his hand comfortingly.

Brandon nodded in agreement. "That's what I was thinking and I know just what we should do. I'll make all of the arrangements to move you and Sweet out of your apartment and into my house in Monterey." His voice reflected his growing excitement.

Sash looked at him in surprise, "Oh, you will?" Brandon didn't notice the lack of excitement in her voice.

Standing, he began to pace. "You're going to need some new things, and I've got to buy Sweet everything. He'll need new clothes. I'll get the decorator to do his room. Oh, the alarm system. I've got to get a new one, a better one. If reporters can get past the old one then anybody can. Oh! I forgot the media. They're going to have a field day with this one. But that's all right. I'll deal with that."

"I'm sure you will." Sash's tone dripped with enough sarcasm to gain Brandon's attention this time.

Feeling uneasy at her tone, Brandon stopped pacing and walked over to Sash. He hunkered down. "Is there a problem? Isn't that what you want? I thought that we cared about each other…"

Sash looked at Brandon. Did the man have a clue that she was falling in love with him? That was a little more than caring. Yet, she had traveled this road before, with a lot less at stake. No one would control her life again.

"I do care about you, Brandon." *Very much.* Sash rose and walked away, afraid that she would say the words out loud. She turned back to face him. "We've been through a lot together in a short time, but what's happening now, your being Sweet's father, it's overwhelming. I've got to have some time to think about all of this."

Brandon rose and went to Sash. "What is there to think about?" He lifted her chin and looked into her eyes. "I want you and Sweet with me."

Sash looked at him steadily. "But what about what *I* want?"

Brandon looked disconcerted. "You don't want to be with me?"

For Sash it was deja vu—the words, the hurt expression. The only difference between this conversation and her last conversation with Michael was that Brandon wanted Sweet. He was his father. He wanted him very much. "It's not about whether I want to be with you, Brandon, it's about me making my *own* decision about what I want. I've only known you for about a month. Anyway, I have other options."

Brandon took a step backward, ready to throw up a shield against yet another rejection. His voice hardened. "What options? You don't have a job. You don't have any money. I'm offering you everything! You can be with Sweet… "

"Be with Sweet?" Sash's voice rose in irritation at the implication in his words. "I'll be with Sweet whether we're living with you or not."

Brandon drew back as if he had been slapped. "Well, he'll be with you for a while, of course, but…"

"*But* nothing! I'm Sweet's legal guardian. I have custody of him and that's the way it is. He lives with me."

Brandon was unable to believe what he was hearing. He cared about this woman more than she would ever know, and she said that she cared for him; but if Sash really cared about him she wouldn't dare stand there and try and deny him his son. He fought his rising anger. "My plan was for the three of us to live together, but if you don't see this as a possibility, then a gradual transition from your house to mine would be best for Sweet, and you can have visitation whenever you want. "

Sash flinched. "Visitation?"

Brandon wanted to bite back the words as soon as he said them. She had hurt him and he wanted to hurt her, but he knew that there was no satisfaction in retaliation. He wanted to reach out, to apologize and take back the veiled threat, but his pride wouldn't let him. After all, she didn't want him, but Sweet was still his son. It was obvious that something would have to be worked out.

Visitation! Sash tried to take a calming breath. She harbored silent fears of this sort of confrontation when Brandon suspected that he was Sweet's uncle. The relationship was even closer now and her fears were no longer silent. Brandon had the nerve to make threats already. Well he could forget it. The thought of losing Sweet seared her heart. She loved this man, but she was not going to be bullied. Sweet belonged to her! Stiffening, her manner became cool and controlled.

"I'm sure that you have your own plans, Brandon, but *I've* decided that Sweet and I will be leaving this island tomorrow so that I can go home and have some time to myself to think about this."

"You're doing what?" Brandon was certain that he had misunderstood. He was wrong.

"I'll make arrangements for the boat to take us off the island and I'll pay for us to fly back to California, if I have to charge it. When you get back to Monterey, we can discuss when *we* can tell Sweet about his relationship to you, as well as *your* visitation arrangements." Walking to the door, she held it open for him to exit. "We appreciate everything you've done for us. Thank you."

Calmly, Brandon walked to the open door and shut it firmly. He stood glaring down at Sash. Defiantly, she returned his glare.

"I'm glad that you *appreciate* what I've done, Sash, but we're not through talking. If you think I'm going to let you take my son off this island before we've settled this matter you're sadly mistaken."

Sash wasn't intimidated. "So you're kidnapping us, Brandon? Is that what you're saying? I hate to tell you, but its been done before. "

Brandon scoffed. "Don't be ridiculous. All I'm saying is that presently you have no job and no prospects. The boy may be doing well now, psychologically, but he still needs to see a therapist after the trauma he's been through. You can't afford that. I want to make certain that Sweet is well taken care of, and I can provide that care. On top of that, tell me how you can protect him when word gets out that he's my son—the only heir to a fortune? Hell, you were snatched off the streets when he was simply your brother. You have no way to protect him. You can't even protect yourself."

Bristling from his verbal attack that held too much truth, Sash stood firm. "Oh really! Well if you try to stop us from leaving this island tomorrow, we'll see who *can't* protect herself!"

Enraged, she rushed to the closet and snatched her suitcase out. Tossing it on the bed, she opened it and started snatching clothing from the dresser drawers, working around Brandon.

Seething, he watched Sash's deliberate movements. Had this woman lost her mind? He couldn't believe that she was serious. "Do you really think that I'm going to let you leave this island?"

"Oh, I'm leaving and you're not stopping me."

"And how is this going to be accomplished if I tell the boat operator not to take you off?"

"If I've got to walk on water I'll be leaving here, and *with* Sweet." She kept on packing.

Brandon was incredulous. How had things gone so wrong? He had such plans for the three of them. "Sash, this is my son we're talking about, a son that I've been denied once and you're telling me that you would take him away from me?"

The agony in Brandon's voice brought Sash's actions to an abrupt halt. She loved this man and hurting him was the last thing she wanted to do. She knew the source of his pain; but her needs had to be respected as well. Brandon's anger was as acute as her own anger, but some rationale had to prevail.

"I could never in good conscience deny Sweet a father, nor deny a father his son, but I won't lie down and become anyone's door mat—not again." Her tone softened. "I'm sure that something can be worked out between us about Sweet, but this is not all about you and what you want, and that's what I've been hearing. I want to make it perfectly clear that I'm the one who has the say so about my life and about Sweet's."

Brandon's jaw tightened with stubborn determination. "We'll see."

Sighing, Sash looked out the window to see the sun rising and then turned back to Brandon. Her emotions were raw. Too much had happened and she didn't feel like fighting with this man. "Yes, Brandon. We will see. Meanwhile, we've both said things to hurt each other and I don't want to hurt you or be hurt anymore. So, I'm going outside to see the sunrise and to take a walk. I need to calm down and so do you. These past few hours have been a roller coaster ride and I've got to find some peace. But I still plan on leaving here tomorrow, whether you like it or not."

That said, Sash left the room, while a tense and angry Brandon watched her walk away.

* * *

Sash felt like the wicked witch from the Wizard of Oz as she marched toward the boat waiting to take her and Sweet to the mainland. The little boy beside her was wailing his protest as loudly as he could. Ahead of her was Brandon on the dock staring daggers at her as she led the child toward him. She stood as the ogre between man and child—father and son—and it wasn't a pleasant place to be. Last night she had faced a resistant Brandon, this morning a resistant little boy. He had made it clear that he didn't want to leave this island, not without Mr. B.

Earlier, when she informed Sweet that they would be going home, she had answered the many questions that he had about why they were leaving as honestly as she could. She told him that it was time for their lives to return to normal. She had to find a job and he had to return to school. None of the reasons were good enough for Sweet. It wasn't until Sash told him that she would miss him too much if she left the island without him that Sweet had quieted down. Yet, he was still reluctant.

As they drew closer to the dock where Brandon stood between her and the boat, Sash's eyes shifted to the man standing beside him. It was John Nathan, with whom she had become all too familiar. So this was it, the promised confrontation. She hoped that there wouldn't be a scene. The fact that the boat was there and waiting at the dock was a plus. But was it waiting for both of them or only for her?

Spotting Brandon, Sweet broke from Sash's grip and took off at a gallop straight toward him. Brandon's firm expression melted as he watched the boy running down the dock at full speed. Bending down, he reached out and swept his son into arms.

"Mr. B, I've been looking for you," Sweet informed him trying to loosen Brandon's vice-like hug. "Sash said that we're leaving the island. Can you come home with us? I don't want to leave without you. "

Brandon swallowed, fighting the sorrow that clutched his heart as he held his son. He had come to the dock to confront Sash, to put her on the boat and send her on her way without Sweet; but as he looked into the innocent face of his child he knew that he couldn't do it. The boy had been through enough. Separating him from his sister this way would be devastating. For the child's sake, he would have to let him go.

He pretended bravado as he told him, "I can't come right now, T, but I'll be coming home soon, and the two of us will go somewhere together when I do I promise." He placed a kiss in the boy's hair and looked at Sash who now stood in front of him. Her stance was clearly challenging, but her eyes softened as he looked into them. For a moment he thought she might change her mind.

Sash felt herself weakening. She loved the man, but... No! She couldn't stay here and she couldn't leave her Sweet with Brandon. She was frightened. He might try to keep him. She might not see him again. Remembering the pain of their previous forced separation, the moment of weakness passed. Slipping on her sunglasses, she took Sweet from Brandon arms into her own. No! She had to go.

"You'll be seeing Mr. B, soon, I'm sure, Sweet. So, come on."

With tears still flowing, Sweet leaned over and kissed Brandon, appeased only by the promise of seeing him again. As the boat moved away from the dock, Sash fought her own tears as the figure of the man she loved grew smaller and smaller until, gradually, it disappeared.

* * *

"I'll crush her!" Brandon stalked the living room like a hungry lion. "I'll take her pretty little butt to court and have her begging for mercy. She can't win. I don't know why she would even try me!"

John Nathan took another sip of his soda. This was his second one in the hour that he had been sitting here listening to Brandon rant. He had been venting since Sash Adams left the island that morning with the boy. John had been relieved that a confrontation had been avoided. He hadn't been looking forward to one, especially in front of the child. As he watched the lady marching toward the waiting boat like a solider ready for battle, he shuddered to think what would have happened if he had tried to stop her as he had been ordered.

John could see Brandon physically trying to restrain himself from snatching the child away from her when she took him, and for a second John thought that Sash would capitulate and allow the boy to stay. He could see by the way she looked at Brandon that her heart wasn't in what she was doing. Pride and a test of wills was involved in the clash between these two strong personalities, as well as unspoken emotions. Any fool could see that she was in love with the man, except Brandon who obviously didn't see it. Or maybe Brandon wasn't looking close enough. The poor sap was so in love with Sash Adams he was practically a basket case.

John took another sip of his drink and sighed. Some of the younger men these days were so inept when it came to women. John had been working for Brandon Plaine for the past three years. He found Brandon to be a kind and decent man, but not one to reveal his emotions. This was the first time since he started working for him that he had seen him so upset by anything, especially by a woman. This was a man who thought he had control of his world, but he woke up one day and found that there were things beyond his control. Sash Adams was one of those. Brandon had no clue how to handle Sash and it was driving him crazy.

John liked the woman. She had spunk, and although he knew it wasn't any of his business it was his opinion that she and Brandon might be good together. So, taking that into consideration he decided to help the man out. He refocused his attention on Brandon who continued his tirade.

"So she did me the magnanimous favor of telling Sweet that he would see me again soon. She can bet that I'll see him again, and I'll see her in court too *very* soon. She'll be putting that Stanford law degree of hers to good use!"

Spent from his emotional tirade, Brandon dropped down beside John.

"Are you through?" John asked Brandon, handing him a soda.

Taking the soft drink from him, Brandon didn't answer. Melancholy began settling over him as quickly as the anger that had risen as he watched Sash and Sweet walk away. They had been gone less than two hours and he missed them both like he would miss a limb.

"You know, Brandon, I loved a woman once the way that you love Sash Adams." John said quietly.

"I'm not in love with Sash," Brandon denied indignantly. "What are you talking about?"

John shook his head at the younger man's indignation and continued. "She was sassy, stubborn, proud and independent. She drove me crazy at every turn. The more I pushed, the more she pulled. The woman drove me batty."

John had Brandon's attention. He had described Sash up and down. "What did you do about it?"

"Well, my father offered me two pieces of advice that worked like a charm."

Brandon looked wary. "What was that?"

"First, you can get more bees with honey and second, compromise won't kill you."

Brandon sighed, disappointed. *Compromise. He had heard that word before*. "That wasn't much of a revelation." He took a sip of his soft drink. "What happened to the woman?'

John finished his soda with a long, slow sip before flashing Brandon a satisfied grin. "She married me."

CHAPTER 18

"He's here! He's here!" Sweet raced from the window seat, whizzed past Sash who was coming down the hallway and disappeared into his room. Sash continued walking toward the living room to await Brandon's knock on the front door. Her heart was racing uncontrollably at the thought of seeing him.

It had been a week since she left Hawaii. She and Brandon had not seen each other since that time. Yet, his generosity remained consistent, providing security to guard the vicinity around Sash's home so that the media that continued to clamor for interviews would not harass her and Sweet. In addition, Brandon called every day. The conversations were usually strained but polite, centering predominantly on Sweet. Neither of them took the opportunity to interject substance into the context of what was said. Their feelings for each other were never discussed, but the distance served to lessen the contention between the two of them.

Brandon's last call had been yesterday when he informed Sash that he would be back in Monterey and that he would like to see Sweet. She had agreed. They had also agreed that they would give father and son more time together before breaking the news of their biological relationship.

His first knock on the front door seemed tentative, but it was followed by a much more confident knock. Taking a fortifying breath, Sash steeled herself for the first glimpse of the man she was trying hard to stop loving.

On the other side of the door, Brandon stood nervously trying to gain control of his runaway heart. The prospect of seeing Sash and spending time alone with Sweet had his stomach tied in knots. He had thought of nothing else but the two of them since they left Pineapple Hill.

His talk with John had given him plenty to think about. He couldn't deny that at times he could be overbearing and he did have a tendency to be a little too controlling. Maybe compromising a bit wouldn't kill him. As a matter of fact, it could probably do him some good learning to compromise with the woman that he loved—and he was in love with Sash Adams. He finally had to admit it to himself. It was a scary proposition, but he was ready to try and love again, try and trust again. He wanted her back in his life. Now, if she would only listen and give him half a chance, he meant to let her know how he felt about her.

When Brandon knocked for entrance the second time, he did so with renewed confidence. The door slowly opened and Sash appeared.

Brandon had to remind himself to breathe. She looked so good. Dressed in a colorful turquoise dress with matching sandals, her shiny locks were held back from her face with an African motif head wrap. Her make up was lightly applied and the small gold hoop earrings reflecting against her brown skin added just the right touch. The scented oil she wore was unrelenting on his senses. Brandon swallowed hard.

"Hello, Sash. It's good to see you."

"Hello, Brandon. It's good to see you, too."

"How are you?"

"Fine. Come on in."

Sash stepped aside for Brandon to enter, bothered by the stiff formality of their greeting. Her stomach fluttered as he passed her. Even dressed casually in a pair of linen shorts and a matching shirt he still looked good. As she closed the door behind Brandon, Sweet came running down the hall and straight into his arms.

"Mr. B!" His exuberant greeting caused both adults to smile with pleasure. "I missed you," he informed Brandon as he planted a kiss on his cheek.

"I missed you, too, T." Brandon hugged the boy close to him. "Man, did I miss you." He buried his nose in the boy's hair and kissed the top of his head.

As Sash watched father and son she asked herself how she could have missed the resemblance between them. As much as Sweet looked like the picture she saw of his Uncle Brice, he looked just as much like Brandon. As Brandon's son, she could see how Sweet could thrive and grow into manhood. This unexpected opportunity was a once in a lifetime chance for him and she had to give him that chance.

Brandon kissed Sweet again and gave him a grin. "Are you ready to spend the weekend with me, bud..." Brandon stopped short as his eyes met Sash's eyes. His voice fell an octave. "Buddy?"

Sweet nodded. "Uh huh. I got clothes in my backpack and Sash gave me some money of my own to spend." Withdrawing a bill from his pocket, Sweet held it up proudly.

Kissing his son a third time, Brandon lowered Sweet to the floor, his arm still around him holding him close, reluctant to let him go. "Good boy. Sash thinks of everything, doesn't she?"

"Uh huh," Sweet agreed with a vigorous shake of his head. "Sash loves me."

Brandon smiled down at Sash. "Yes," he said softly. "Sash is full of love."

The words were said tenderly, touching her heart as surely as if Brandon had reached inside and caressed it. Her eyes held his and she knew that his next words were meant only for her.

"I wonder how far that love can extend?" Brandon took a step toward her. "Could it reach far enough to for…"

The ring of the telephone startled both Brandon and Sash out of their mutual trances. Impatient at the interruption, Sash excused herself and answered the call with an abrupt, "Hello."

An accented voice greeted her on the other end. "Hello, Sash, It's Michael."

"Hello, Michael." Out of the corner of her eye she noticed Brandon react to the name she had spoken.

Michael! Michael Ramuba was calling Sash! Brandon could feel the heat rising from the pit of his stomach. The fire that had been in his eyes for Sash instantly turned to a stony glare. Taking Sweet by the hand, he led the way to the door. "Come on, T. We've got to go." With his little boy in tow Brandon left Sash's apartment without a backward glance or a farewell.

* * *

Brandon didn't want to remember what his world had been like before Sweet came into his life. While he had enjoyed the time spent with him when they were in Hawaii, being alone with his son magnified the pleasure. The boy's personality was totally endearing and Brandon was fascinated by everything he did. Sweet was funny, bright, curious and compassionate. He was everything that any man could want in his child. By the end of their first evening together Brandon had come to the conclusion that his son was a genius and he was considering having him tested.

As he tucked Sweet into bed in a room that Brandon had turned into a virtual toy store, he was reluctant to let the boy go to sleep. He wanted to sit in the room and marvel at the miracle that he had helped create, just as he had done in Hawaii. He didn't want to miss one more day, hour, minute or second of Sweet's young life. But the word compromise was in serious jeopardy when Brandon heard Michael's name coming from Sash's lips—lips that had driven him into a frenzy only days before. Well, he wasn't going to have it. He would not tolerate another man in his son's life! If Sash wanted Michael Ramuba she could have him, but Sweet would not grow up under any man's influence but his own.

"Are you thinking about my sister, Mr. B?" Sweet asked behind a yawn.

Brandon started at the question and the boy's intuitiveness. "Why do you ask that?" Brandon hedged.

"Cause you like her," Sweet said burrowing under the down comforter covered with his favorite cartoon characters. "And she likes you." He turned on his side and got comfortable. "I told you that before, Mr. B. She likes you better than Mr. Mike."

Brandon was on instant alert. Was it inappropriate to

pump a child? Probably, but he wasn't going to let that stop him.

"What do you mean by that, T?" He tried to sound nonchalant.

"Huh?" Came the sleepy reply as Sweet started to drift off to sleep.

Brandon bit his lip trying to stop himself from shaking him awake. After all the child needed his rest. On second thought he would let him sleep late tomorrow. Lightly, he shook his shoulder. "What do you mean when you said that Sash likes me better than Mr. Mike? Did she tell you that?"

Sweet peered at Brandon through drooping eyes that threatened to close in a second, "Sash likes you, you like Sash and Mr. Mike likes Sash. He told me…" Sweet gave a wide yawn that for Brandon seemed to go on forever. As the yawn diminished in degrees Sweet's eyes began to close accordingly. Brandon grew desperate.

"He told you what? What did Mr. Mike tell you?"

"I talked to him on the telephone and he told me that he would like to be my new Daddy." With that slurred declaration Sweet drifted off to sleep, while Brandon stood by his bedside in shock.

* * *

"I know that I've made mistakes with us, Sash," Michael's voice was soft and seductive. But my feelings for you aren't a mistake. I still love you, and I probably always will. I nearly went out of my mind when I read what had happened to you and your brother. I need to see you, sweetheart. Please. Tell me what I can do to make what I've done up to you, darling, and I'll do it. I promise I will."

Sash switched the telephone from one ear to another as she lounged on the couch in her living room. She had been talking to this man for one solid hour, which was fifty-five minutes too long. This was his second call to her today, and she should have hung up when he called her back.

At one time Michael's words would have been all that Sash needed to hear. She would have forgiven him and returned to his arms. She had done it before, too many times. But that had been two years ago. The love she once felt for him no longer existed and his hollow promises fell on deaf ears. She needed to put an end to this.

Sash tried to measure her words carefully. "Michael, we've been through the romantic stage in our lives and I've told you, I'd just like for us to be…"

"Friends," Michael finished her sentence with a snarl. She could almost see the scowl on his face. "Please, Sash, don't insult me. That has to be the oldest rejection line in the world in any language."

Sash heard the misery in Michael's heavy sigh. Anyone who saw Michael would think that she was insane for rejecting him. He was handsome, suave and sophisticated. His family's wealth afforded him the opportunity to be educated in three countries: England, France and the United States. He had his pick of women from all over the world who would welcome his attention; but Sash had enjoyed it, suffered through it and no longer wanted it. That was what he didn't seem to understand.

"It's over Michael and has been for a long time. You have to accept that."

"Is it Brandon Plaine? Is that the reason you no longer care for me?" Michael's voice was tinged with anger.

Sash was determined in her resolve. "I care for you,

Michael. We've been special in each other's lives and I'll never forget that. But I'm trying to be honest with you. I don't feel the same way about you that I did two years ago."

Michael wouldn't relent. "But you feel something for Brandon Plaine, am I correct?"

"Brandon and I went through a lot together and we've become friends."

"The question is how close are you as *friends*. Closer than you want to be with me, that's for certain."

Michael's attitude was getting increasingly annoying. It was time to put an end to this conversation.

"Michael, I've got to go. I think it best that you don't call me again and that we don't see each other. Thank you for your concern. Good-bye." She disconnected the call. That chapter in her life had ended a long time ago. It would not be resurrected.

Sash was about to go back to her room when the telephone rang again. She was tempted to let it ring. It might be Michael again. Then she remembered that Sweet was with Brandon and thought it best to answer the call.

"Hello, Adams residence."

"Yes, Sash. It's Brandon."

He didn't sound like himself. Sash's heart skipped a beat "What's wrong? Is something wrong with Sweet?" She prepared herself to hear the worse.

"Sweet is doing just fine, but I'm not. I want you over here right away." Brandon's voice hardened. "And I mean *now!*"

CHAPTER 19

"What in the world is your problem, Brandon, feeding a child candy at 9:00 in the morning? I don't allow Sweet to eat candy and midnight is too late for a five year old to go to bed!" Sash was incensed. She had gone to pick Sweet up from his weekend with Brandon to find the child munching on a chocolate candy bar and exhausted as the result of having stayed up until the early morning hours watching videos.

Brandon looked contrite, but he tried to defend the indefensible anyway. "Whoever heard of a child not having candy? Anyway, he had breakfast first and he wanted to see the movies last night." He had to admit that both arguments did sound weak, but that didn't stop him from trying.

"That's not the point. You can't let him do what he wants when he wants to. He's a little kid. You're the adult."

"Well, I don't see how one chocolate bar is going to kill him." Brandon huffed. Turning he strolled away, aware that their disagreement wasn't really about a candy bar and Sweet's bedtime. First of all, he had called her two days ago to come to his home and she was just arriving. Secondly, he didn't appreciate his request having been ignored.

Sash followed Brandon, stopping short at the entrance to the living room. Her eyes widened in disbelief. The expensive Berber carpeting was covered with toys from one end of the room to the other.

"What in the world is all this?" Her eyes circled the room. There were toy stores not as well stocked as Brandon's living room. Every toy imaginable was on display. "This is ridiculous. No one child can play with all of this stuff."

"Sweet and I sure tried. He even took a spin around the house in his new electric car." Brandon managed to find a pair of leather loafers abandoned among the clutter. He slipped his bare feet into them. "And getting back to his bedtime, one late evening won't hurt him either."

Brandon's parenting style was a bit too permissive for Sash. "There are rules in child-raising, Brandon, that simply shouldn't be ignored. A child has to have boundaries."

"You can impose those tomorrow. This weekend was about Sweet and me getting to know each other and having a good time." Tossing a few toys aside, he settled on the sofa. "Right now we have more important things to talk about." He patted the empty space beside him for Sash. Ignoring the familiar gesture, Sash took a seat in the chair opposite where he was sitting. She didn't want to be the least bit distracted by her attraction to him.

"You'd better talk fast, Sweet will be down in a minute." Sash settled back in her seat and crossed her legs. That simple action turned Brandon's brain waves into sawdust as the shorts she was wearing moved up her shapely legs. All he could think of was how those legs had locked around his body as they made love on a rainy day.

Brandon's nonchalance was deceptive. He had been in a jealous rage when she didn't appear at his house after his call to her. He wanted to storm over to her house and demand an explanation about her relationship with Michael. Only fear of what he might find when he got there stopped him from going to confront her. Michael's car might be there. He might have even spent the night. He hated the jealousy that he was feeling, but this was the woman that he loved. This was the only woman who had ever continuously challenged him. The only woman who had ever made him lose control. The thought that she might be making love to Michael had kept him up long after he had tucked Sweet into bed each night.

In his heart he sensed that Sash was a one-man woman, and he wanted to be that man. Yet she had been in love with Michael and she wasn't in love with him. For the first time in his life Brandon was faced with a situation that he wasn't sure how to solve. How could he make her love him?

Sash sat across from Brandon swinging one leg impatiently over the other oblivious to the effect that she was having on him. He appeared to be daydreaming and she had things to do.

"Brandon, what do you want?"

Sash's impatient voice jolted him out of his meditative state. "What? What did you say?"

Sash started to rise. "You're not even listening to me. I don't have time for this."

"No! I'm sorry. I'm listening. Sit back."

Sash did so, but continued to give him a piece of her mind. "You ordered me over here the other day as if I were a slave. Then when I didn't *obey* you called back and had the nerve to get even more obnoxious, leaving messages on my answering machine. You should know by now that I won't jump to your command. If there was nothing wrong with

Sweet there was no need for me to come over here until I had to. Now I'm here. What is it that is *so* important?"

"I'm going to tell Sweet that I'm his father and I'm going to do it today."

The words blurted without preamble had Sash gaping at him open mouthed. "Today? Now? Isn't that a little soon?"

"I don't see any reason to wait. I'll still be his father whether it's today or ten years from now. Is there a reason that you don't want me to tell him now?"

Sash grasped at straw. She wanted a little bit longer with her brother, a little more time for them to be together before everything changed.

"But I think that he needs to get to know you better before we tell him. I don't want to confuse him. Why do you think that it has to be today?" She tried not to sound desperate, but she did, and she was.

Brandon caught the catch in her voice. He had been prepared to play hardball, but the wounded timbre in her voice took the feeling of satisfaction out of his reply. "It has to be now because I don't appreciate Michael Ramuba telling my son that he wants to be his Daddy."

"What!" The revelation brought Sash to her feet.

Maybe she didn't know. Brandon came to his feet as well. "That's what Sweet told me. Michael said that to him in a telephone conversation that they seemed to have had."

"Believe me, Brandon. This is the first I've heard about this!"

She didn't know! Brandon smiled inwardly.

"Sweet answered the telephone the other day when Michael first called and I was in the shower, but I didn't know that they had any kind of conversation. Sweet never told me. The nerve of Michael!"

'The nerve of Michael!' Yes! That didn't sound like a woman falling back in love. "Well, I don't want another man trying to take my place."

"There's no argument with that. Believe me, Michael would never be the one to take your place."

Double yes!

Sash was on a roll and Brandon loved it as she threatened to call Michael and give him a piece of her mind. She recounted how Michael tried to dominate her.

Oh, oh. That sounded familiar. That was a mistake he no longer intended to make.

The more Brandon heard about Sash's opinion of her relationship with Michael the better he felt. Michael Ramuba was definitely not a barrier to his pursuit of Sash, but that didn't mean that another man might not be in the future. He didn't want any other man in Sweet's life, nor in Sash's either. This was a woman whose love and care for his son was absolute. She was strong and smart, to say nothing of being beautiful. Any man would want her, but he was determined not to give any other man that chance.

"I'm glad to hear that Michael is out of the picture," Brandon confessed once Sash ran out of steam. "I was worried when I heard you on the telephone with him. I was jealous."

Sash stilled as the atmosphere in the room began to shift. "Jealous? Why would you be jealous?" Her voice wavered at the possibilities.

Brandon turned up the heat, moving closer to Sash. He left little room between them and no doubts about his intentions. "Because you have a history with him and I want you to have a beginning with me."

She could hardly breathe. "Oh yeah? On what terms?"

"On any term you want." Brandon whispered. "I'm willing to compromise." Hands still at his sides, he planted a light kiss on her tempting lips.

Sash filled her lungs with air, then expelled slowly. "Why have you come to this conclusion so suddenly?"

Brandon brushed a stray lock away from her face. "There's nothing sudden about how I feel about you, Sash. It's been growing steadily each day." He took a breath of courage. "I love you and I want you to know it."

Sash was speechless. She felt as if the world suddenly stopped spinning.

Brandon continued. "As a matter of fact, I have a little something for you."

Sash watched as if in a fog as Brandon crossed the room and withdrew a small package from the pocket of his jacket. It was wrapped in gold foil and tied with a red satin ribbon. Returning to Sash, he handed it to her.

"I brought it to the house to give to you as a peace offering the day I came to pick up Sweet, but you were preoccupied."

Still recovering from Brandon's earth shattering confession, mechanically Sash unwrapped the package. She opened the wooden box beneath the wrapping, inside, resting on a velvet lining lay a gold plated Cartier writing pen. Her name was engraved on it in script. Sash's hand flew to her chest. "Oh, Brandon! It's beautiful."

Brandon grinned at the pleasure on her face. "It's just a little something to replace the pen the authorities couldn't find at the house where they kept you. A new pen for what I hope can be a new beginning. I'm sorry about what happened in the past, Sash. I never meant to disrespect you. I do love you. I love everything about you. I hope that you can forgive me and that we can start over."

Sash examined the exquisite gift, touched by the thoughtfulness behind the gesture and the sincerity behind his words. Brandon was letting her know that he was ready for a relationship based on mutual respect. That was all she had asked for, all that she wanted. If he was willing take a big step forward, so was she.

Closing the gap between them, she kissed him with a thoroughness that left them both breathless. "I love you, too, Brandon, and I'm more than ready for a new beginning. And it can start by your telling Sweet that you're his Daddy."

"He's my Daddy?"

The small voice from the doorway propelled both adults to whirl around to pinpoint its source. Sweet stood in the living room entrance holding a tennis shoe in each hand. His eyes were as round as saucers as they traveled from adult to adult. The debate as to when to tell Sweet about his parentage was over. Like it or not, it had been taken out of their hands.

"I thought our Daddy was in heaven, Sash?" he asked, his gaze finally settling on her. "How can Mr. B be my Daddy? He's not the man in the picture."

His reference was to the picture of James and Mildred Curry that sat on Sweet's nightstand. Each night after saying his prayers, his ritual was to kiss the picture. How was this drastic change in his young life to be explained to the child.. Sash stood rooted, unsure of what to do or say.

It was Brandon who took the lead. Going over to the child, he picked him up, carried him over to the sofa and sat down. Settling Sweet on his lap, he took one of the shoes out of his hands and began the mundane task of putting Sweet's shoe on his foot. Snapping out of her trance, Sash joined them on the sofa where Brandon handed her the other shoe, a silent signal for her to follow his course of action.

"I'm sure that Sash, can explain the picture, T." Brandon nodded, encouraging her to do so. As she did, her approach to the delicate subject became as casual as the action of working Sweet's foot into his shoe.

"The Daddy in the picture was the one you and I shared before he went to heaven," she explained as she went about her task.

Brandon worked the little boy's foot into his other shoe. "And I'm your Daddy right here on earth from now on, yours alone. You're my son."

Sash confirmed Brandon's words with a smile. "That's right, sweetheart. Our Daddy who went to heaven with our mother took care of you until Mr. B could come and get you."

Finishing the shoe-tying task with a flourish, Brandon made it all sound so simple. "You want to know something, son? Your other Daddy loved you and so did your mother, just like Sash and I do." He hugged the boy to him and gave him a kiss. "Man, you are so lucky. God gave you two Daddies. Every little boy can't be that lucky."

Sweet sat between them silently for a moment, appearing to ponder what had been said. Finally, crossing his arms across his small chest, he nodded in agreement. "Yeah, I am a lucky boy." He turned to Brandon. "So, Mr. B can I call you Daddy, too?"

The request took Brandon by surprise. Too choked to reply, he nodded.

As Sweet gave his new-found father a hug, Sash smiled at the two of them. Brandon's words had been the right words. His approach had been the right one and Sweet had been accepting. Maybe things would work out after all.

CHAPTER 20

Sash sat in Brandon's Monterey office watching him as he conducted the telephone conference with his staff in San Francisco. How different this visit was compared to the last one she made to his office. That was only three months ago, but it seemed like a lifetime. No longer were she and Brandon two frantic strangers reluctantly bonded together by the fate of a child. Things were much different now. As Brandon reached out, took her hand and tugged her from the chair in which she was sitting and onto his lap, the hard evidence of that difference was evident. She gave a little wiggle, followed by a sensual smile.

"Tease," Brandon whispered hotly in her ear as he nuzzled the slender column of her neck. The conference call on his speakerphone was all but forgotten.

Sash proceeded to show him how much of a tease she could be as she took the tip of his ear lobe between her teeth and gave it a light tug. The slight graze of her tongue on the offended spot nearly brought Brandon out of his chair and her tumbling off his lap onto the floor.

"Not appropriate for a CEO," she whispered amused at his gallant efforts to bite back a groan of pleasure.

"I love you," Brandon mouthed, tightening his hold around her waist and drawing her closer to him.

"I love you, too." Sash mouthed back, wrapping her arms around his neck and snuggling against him. Thank goodness he wasn't having a video conference.

So much had changed in their lives in so short a time. The best of those changes had started the day that Sweet discovered that Brandon was his father. From the day Mr. B became "Daddy," man and boy bonded as father and son.

Brandon was a fantastic father, just as Sash knew he would be. He had even cut back on his workload to be with his son. He was there at every turn for Sweet and the boy worshipped him.

The question of Sweet's custody was no longer an issue. She and Brandon shared that responsibility. They worked together to provide Sweet with the love and security he needed. In the process the love between Brandon and her grew. They saw each other nearly every day. There were occasional quibbles over minor issues involving Sweet, but when it came to the important ones in the child's life, they were a well-oiled machine. Life was good. She had a new job as a staff attorney at the Poverty Law Center in Salinas, only a short drive from Monterey. With Brandon's help she had a new apartment, located in nearby Carmel. The building was quiet, secluded and provided the security that made both her and Sweet feel safer. And, she had Brandon Plaine. She loved the man and he loved her and they both loved a little boy called, Sweet.

Brandon felt Sash's body relax against his as she sighed in absolute contentment. He could feel his manhood rise.

Conducting a conference call with the woman that you love on your lap wasn't something he would recommend, but who cared. The priorities in his life had shifted so dramatically since Sash and Sweet came into his life that work was far down on his list. The woman in his arms and the child whose love they shared had taken the place of everything else.

As she cuddled up against him, Brandon's hands roamed with purpose under Sash's tee-shirt and caressed her hardened nipples. The voices coming over the speakerphone faded into the background, as he found the front clasp of her bra, and released it. Giving her a kiss that left no doubt as to where it would lead, he shifted her in his arms positioning her to straddle him. Damn the conference call! He could reschedule it. Brandon was about to push the disconnect button ending the call when Sash caught his hand.

"Business before pleasure," she whispered against his lips. Despite his muffled protest, she slid off of Brandon's lap. Standing, Sash secured her bra. She had business of her own to attend to at the moment and if she stayed in his office any longer neither one of them would get anything done. She had left her briefcase in the secretary's outer office when she entered the building and there were some papers that needed her attention. She threw Brandon a kiss as she breezed out of his office door. Catching it, he placed it on his lips with a smile that promised her that their personal business was far from over.

Mrs. Joseph was busy at her computer as Sash entered her office space. She barely noticed Sash's entrance. Finding her briefcase, Sash decided to conduct her business in the assistant's office to give Brandon the opportunity to finish his call. She settled in one of the comfortable chairs reserved for guests.

"How's the new job going, Ms. Adams?" Mrs. Joseph's eyes never left the computer screen.

Sash was startled by the acknowledgment of her presence by the older woman. She was even more startled by the question. She'd only been working for a couple of weeks.

"How did you know about my new job?" Sash asked. This was only the second time she had seen this woman in her life. She was certain that Brandon wasn't spreading her business.

"I saw the announcement in the Salinas newspaper the other day that you had joined the staff at the Poverty Law Center there. Congratulations."

Sash flashed an appreciative smile. "Thank you. It's what I was looking for in practicing law." And it was. She could barely express the satisfaction she felt in fighting for justice for people who could not afford legal assistance. "And Brandon tells me that you'll be moving back to the San Francisco office soon, Mrs. Joseph."

"Yes," she nodded, still typing. "His regular assistant will be back from her leave of absence tomorrow."

Sash withdrew the papers from her briefcase. "Well, I'm sure Brandon will miss you. He says that you're very efficient." Sash took her special pen from its holder and began to sign the papers.

"I'm glad that he thinks so." Mrs. Joseph got up from the computer and crossed the room to the file cabinets. Opening the file drawer she glanced at Sash who was busy signing papers.

"I see that you've got another gold pen." Mrs. Joseph

filed the folder she was carrying, then walked briskly back to her desk. She returned to the computer screen.

Having completed her task, Sash gathered her papers, stacked them neatly in her briefcase and returned her pen to its honored place. Tucking the briefcase casually under her arm, she walked to Brandon's door and re-entered without knocking. It wasn't until she closed the door behind her that her shaking legs threatened to give way. Leaning against the office door, she shut her eyes to regain her composure. When she opened them again Brandon was staring at her looking worried. He started to speak when Sash put a finger to her lips silencing him.

Tossing her briefcase aside, Sash hurried over to Brandon's desk, scribbled a note on a piece of paper and with shaking hands placed it in front of him. Brandon read it. His eyes flew to Sash. There were a million questions in his eyes, but the look on her face caused him to spring into action. He addressed the employee in his San Francisco office heading the conference call. "Ross, I want you to contact John Nathan, ASAP. Tell him to get some security people over here to my office in Monterey fast! And I mean *fast*!"

Disconnecting the call, he took a trembling Sash into his arms. "It's all right, baby. I promise you, it's going to be all right."

* * *

John glanced at Sash Adams as Mrs. Joseph was being led away in handcuffs. "That was some darn good detective work, Ms. Adams. We need you on our security team."

Brandon came up behind Sash and wrapped her in his

arms. "I'm afraid not, John. I've got other plans for this lady." He placed a kiss on her temple.

"Oh, yeah?" Sash raised a curious brow. "Like what?"

Brandon smiled at her mischievously. "Oh, a little something that involves a ring and roses. That is, if that's what you want." Brandon quickly amended. This compromising was still kind of new.

Sash grinned. "We'll see."

John smiled at them both. It seemed like these two might be on the right track.

"Well all I know is that you put the cap on your brother's kidnap case, Ms. Adams." John continued. "I know that I didn't suspected that Charlene Joseph was in on it. The FBI suspected that the abductors got Brandon's private numbers through some glitch in the telephone company. It happens. We checked this Joseph woman out thoroughly and there was never any indication that she knew Monee Sherman or that she had a romantic relationship with Louis Carlton; but she confessed that she was in love with him. It looks like he was playing both women."

"Well, she was a cool one, that's for sure," said Brandon. "I know that it never dawned on me that she was checking on us when she came into the office the day we were here waiting for the ransom call. She sure fooled me." He tightened his arms around Sash, "But this lady here sure hit the mark."

"Her big mistake was mentioning my gold pen," Sash explained. "The authorities never found the pen. The media never knew about it. Either Mrs. Joseph was in that basement and saw the pen there, or one of the kidnappers had to tell her about my stabbing that man with it to escape. How else would she know? If she had kept her mouth shut about it she might have gotten away with everything. I wouldn't have had a clue that she was involved."

After John and the authorities left, Brandon pulled Sash into his office to finish what they had started earlier. Feathering her with kisses, his voice was a low sexy growl as he slid Sash's tee-shirt over her head and tossed it to the floor. "Woman it seems that every time you come into this office you bring some drama with you."

"Oh yeah?" Returning his kisses, Sash wrapped her arms around his body and pressed herself against him. "I guess that's a sacrifice you're going to have to make for loving me, Mr. Plaine."

"I guess I will." Brandon agreed walking them back toward the couch that they planned on using quite creatively. "And what a sweet sacrifice that will be."

THE END

AUTHOR BIOGRAPHY

Crystal Rhodes is a native of Indianapolis, Indiana where she lives with her daughter. A playwright as well as novelist, she has written 19 plays that have been produced in theatres across the United States. Her controversial first novel, *Sin* — the story of a woman minister who falls in love with a man involved in the drug trade — has received critical acclaim.

Ms. Rhodes holds a B.A. degree in social work from Indiana University and a M.A. degree in Sociology from Atlanta University. *Sweet Sacrifice* is her second novel. Look for the release of her third novel *Small Sensations* soon.

Ms. Rhodes invites readers to visit her web site at: www.crystalrhodes.com. She also welcomes your comments at: P.O. Box 53511, Indianapolis, IN 46253 (enclose a stamped, self-addressed envelope if you would like a reply)

SNEAK PREVIEW

New novel by Crystal Rhodes

SMALL SENSATIONS

Davia Maxwell is a street smart, survivor who has clawed her way out of one of Chicago's roughest ghettos to become the owner of Small Sensations, one of the largest manufacturers of children's clothing in the country. A savvy entrepreneur, Davia is strong, intelligent, beautiful and rich. She is also a thirty-four year old grandmother.

Having survived a childhood trauma and the tragic death of her teenage daughter, Davia is a woman scarred by a past that has left her emotionally numb. With the exception of her granddaughter, Gaby, and her business, there is room for nothing else in her life, until she meets Justin Miles, a member of one of the wealthiest African-American families in Atlanta. His mother, Katherine, is the grand dame of Atlanta's black society, and a thirty-four year old grandmother from the ghetto is not a criterion for admission to her social circle or to the Miles family. Katherine vows that Davia Maxwell will never be admitted to either.

ORDER FORM

Crystal Ink Publishing
P.O. Box 53511
Indianapolis, Indiana 46253

Name: ____

Address: ____

City: ____________________________ State ____ Zip________

_____ # of Copies of *Sweet Sacrifice* @ $11.95 per copy

$ ______________

INDIANA RESIDENTS ONLY add 5% sales tax: ______________

Shipping & Handling
(Add $3.00 for the first book) ______________

Additional Shipping & Handling Cost
($1.00 each additional book) ______________

TOTAL AMOUNT DUE $ ______________

Make check or money order out to: Crystal Ink

Mail to: **Crystal Ink Publishing**
P.O. Box 53511
Indianapolis, IN 46253